the GARFIELD show

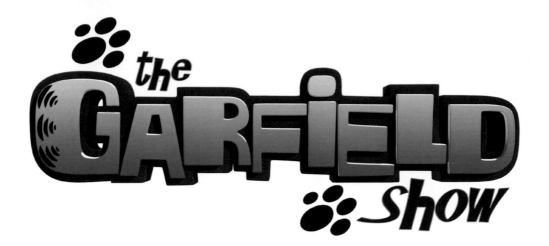

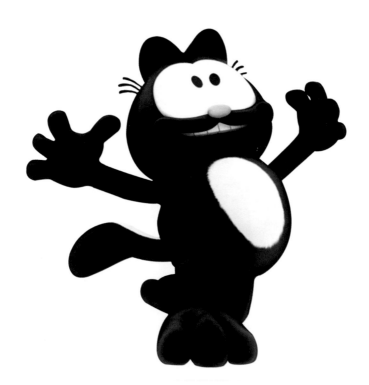

PAPERCUTZ™

GARFIELD GRAPHIC NOVELS AVAILABLE FROM PAPERCUTZ™

GARFIELD
FISH TO FRY
& Co
PAPERCUTZ
GARFIELD & Co #1
"FISH TO FRY"

GARFIELD
THE CURSE OF THE CAT PEOPLE
& Co
PAPERCUTZ
GARFIELD & Co #2
"THE CURSE OF THE CAT PEOPLE"

GARFIELD
CATZILLA
& Co
PAPERCUTZ
GARFIELD & Co #3
"CATZILLA"

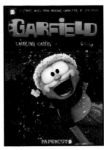

GARFIELD
CAROLING CAPERS
& Co
PAPERCUTZ
GARFIELD & Co #4
"CAROLING CAPERS"

GARFIELD
A GAME OF CAT AND MOUSE
PAPERCUTZ
GARFIELD & Co #5
"A GAME OF CAT AND MOUSE"

GARFIELD
MOTHER GARFIELD
& Co
PAPERCUTZ
GARFIELD & Co #6
"MOTHER GARFIELD"

GARFIELD
HOME FOR THE HOLIDAYS
& Co
PAPERCUTZ
GARFIELD & Co #7
"HOME FOR THE HOLIDAYS"

GARFIELD
SECRET AGENT X
& Co
PAPERCUTZ
GARFIELD & Co #8
"SECRET AGENT X"

GARFIELD
Show
UNFAIR WEATHER
PAPERCUTZ
THE GARFIELD SHOW #1
"UNFAIR WEATHER"

the GARFIELD Show
JON'S NIGHT OUT
PAPERCUTZ
THE GARFIELD SHOW #2
"JON'S NIGHT OUT"

the GARFIELD Show
LONG LOST LYMAN
PAPERCUTZ
THE GARFIELD SHOW #3
"LONG LOST LYMAN"

the GARFIELD Show
LITTLE TROUBLE IN BIG CHINA
PAPERCUTZ
THE GARFIELD SHOW #4
"LITTLE TROUBLE IN BIG CHINA"

the GARFIELD Show
FIDO FOOD FELINE
PAPERCUTZ
THE GARFIELD SHOW #5
"FIDO FOOD FELINE"

the GARFIELD Show
APPRENTICE SORCERER
PAPERCUTZ
THE GARFIELD SHOW #6
"APPRENTICE SORCERER"

GARFIELD & Co GRAPHIC NOVELS ARE AVAILABLE IN HARDCOVER ONLY FOR $7.99 EACH. THE GARFIELD SHOW GRAPHIC NOVELS ARE $7.99 IN PAPERBACK, AND $11.99 IN HARDCOVER EXCEPT #4, #5, AND #6, $12.99 HARDCOVER. AVAILABLE FROM BOOKSELLERS EVERYWHERE.

YOU CAN ALSO ORDER ONLINE FROM PAPERCUTZ.COM OR CALL 1-800-886-1223, MONDAY THROUGH FRIDAY, 9 - 5 EST. MC, VISA, AND AMEX ACCEPTED. TO ORDER BY MAIL, PLEASE ADD $4.00 FOR POSTAGE AND HANDLING FOR FIRST BOOK ORDERED, $1.00 FOR EACH ADDITIONAL BOOK, AND MAKE CHECK PAYABLE TO NBM PUBLISHING. SEND TO: PAPERCUTZ, 160 BROADWAY, SUITE 700, EAST WING, NEW YORK, NY 10038.

GARFIELD & Co AND THE GARFIELD SHOW GRAPHIC NOVELS ARE ALSO AVAILABLE WHEREVER E-BOOKS ARE SOLD.

the GARFIELD show

#6 "APPRENTICE SORCERER"

BASED ON THE ORIGINAL CHARACTERS CREATED BY

JIM DAVIS

PAPERCUTZ™

NEW YORK

THE GARFIELD SHOW #6 "APPRENTICE SORCERER"

"THE GARFIELD SHOW" SERIES © 2016- DARGAUD MEDIA. ALL RIGHTS RESERVED.
© PAWS. "GARFIELD" & GARFIELD CHARACTERS TM & © PAWS INC. - ALL
RIGHTS RESERVED. THE GARFIELD SHOW—A DARGAUD MEDIA PRODUCTION.
IN ASSOCIATION WITH FRANCE3 WITH THE PARTICIPATION OF CENTRE NATIONAL
DE LA CINÉMATOGRAPHIE AND THE SUPPORT OF REGION ILE-DE-FRANCE.
A SERIES DEVELOPED BY PHILIPPE VIDAL, ROBERT REA AND STEVE BALISSAT.
BASED UPON THE CHARACTERS CREATED BY JIM DAVIS. ORIGINAL STORIES:
"STINK, STANK, STUNK," "BARKING MAD," AND "APPRENTICE SORCERER"
(ORIGINALLY "BEWITCHED") WRITTEN BY JULIEN MAGNAT; "BULLDOG OF DOOM"
WRITTEN BY SAMUEL BARKSDALE.

CEDRIC MICHIELS - COMICS ADAPTATION
JOE JOHNSON - TRANSLATIONS
TONY ISABELLA - DIALOGUE RESTORATION
TOM ORZECHOWSKI - LETTERING
JEFF WHITMAN - PRODUCTION COORDINATOR
BETHANY BRYAN - ASSOCIATE EDITOR
JIM SALICRUP
EDITOR-IN-CHIEF

ISBN: 978-1-62991-449-7 PAPERBACK EDITION
ISBN: 978-1-62991-450-3 HARDCOVER EDITION

PRINTED IN CHINA
FEBRUARY 2016 BY TOPPAN LEEFUNG PRINTING LIMITED
JIN JU GUAN LI QU,
DA LING SHAN TOWN,
DONGGUAN, PRC
CHINA

PAPERCUTZ BOOKS MAY BE PURCHASED FOR BUSINESS OR PROMOTIONAL USE. FOR INFORMATION ON
BULK PURCHASES PLEASE CONTACT MACMILLAN CORPORATE AND PREMIUM SALES DEPARTMENT AT
(800) 221-7945 X5442.

DISTRIBUTED BY MACMILLAN
FIRST PAPERCUTZ PRINTING

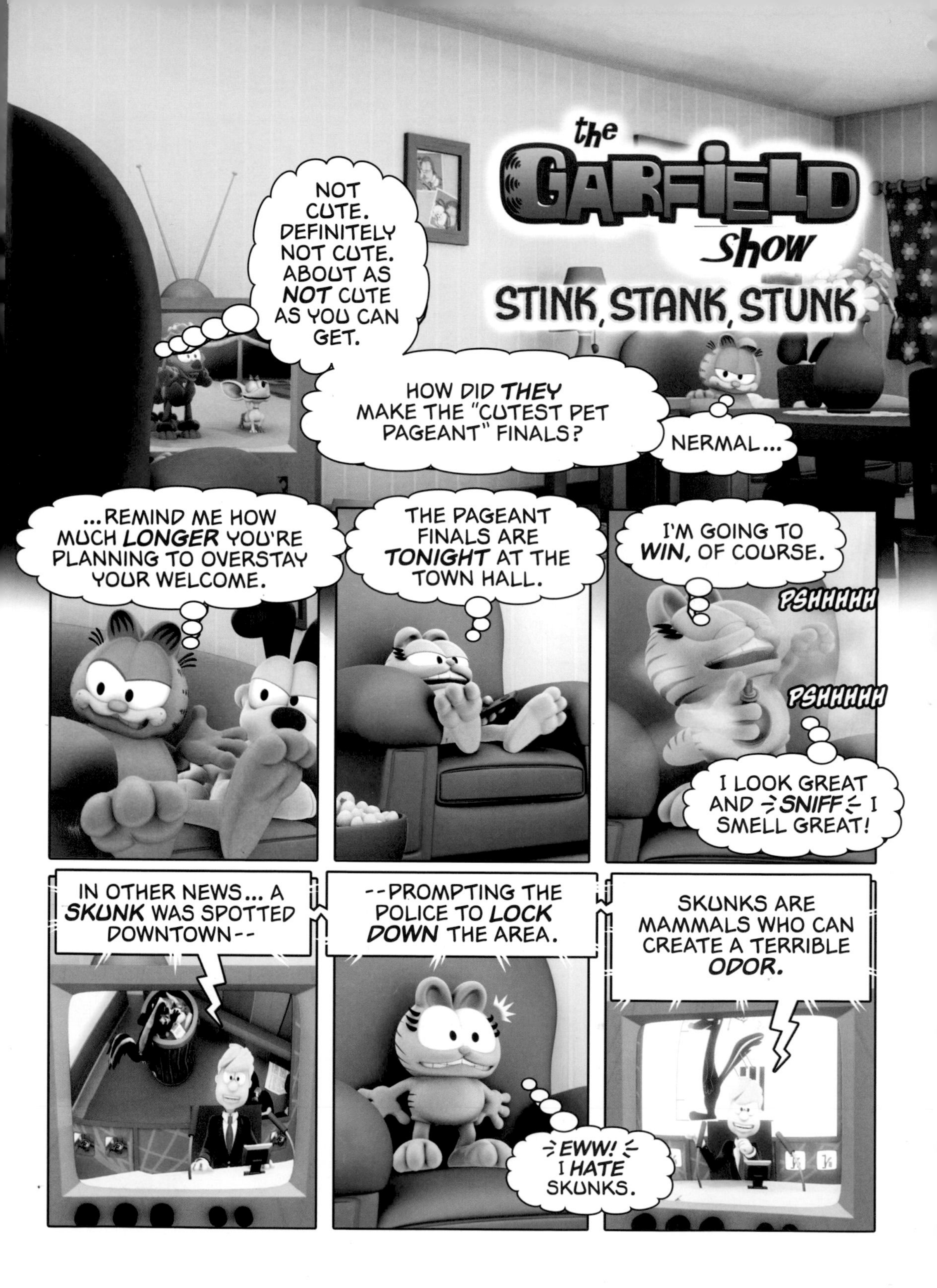
the GARFIELD show
STINK, STANK, STUNK
NOT CUTE. DEFINITELY NOT CUTE. ABOUT AS NOT CUTE AS YOU CAN GET.
HOW DID THEY MAKE THE "CUTEST PET PAGEANT" FINALS?
NERMAL...
...REMIND ME HOW MUCH LONGER YOU'RE PLANNING TO OVERSTAY YOUR WELCOME.
THE PAGEANT FINALS ARE TONIGHT AT THE TOWN HALL.
I'M GOING TO WIN, OF COURSE.
PSHHHHH
PSHHHHH
I LOOK GREAT AND SNIFF I SMELL GREAT!
IN OTHER NEWS... A SKUNK WAS SPOTTED DOWNTOWN--
--PROMPTING THE POLICE TO LOCK DOWN THE AREA.
EWW! I HATE SKUNKS.
SKUNKS ARE MAMMALS WHO CAN CREATE A TERRIBLE ODOR.

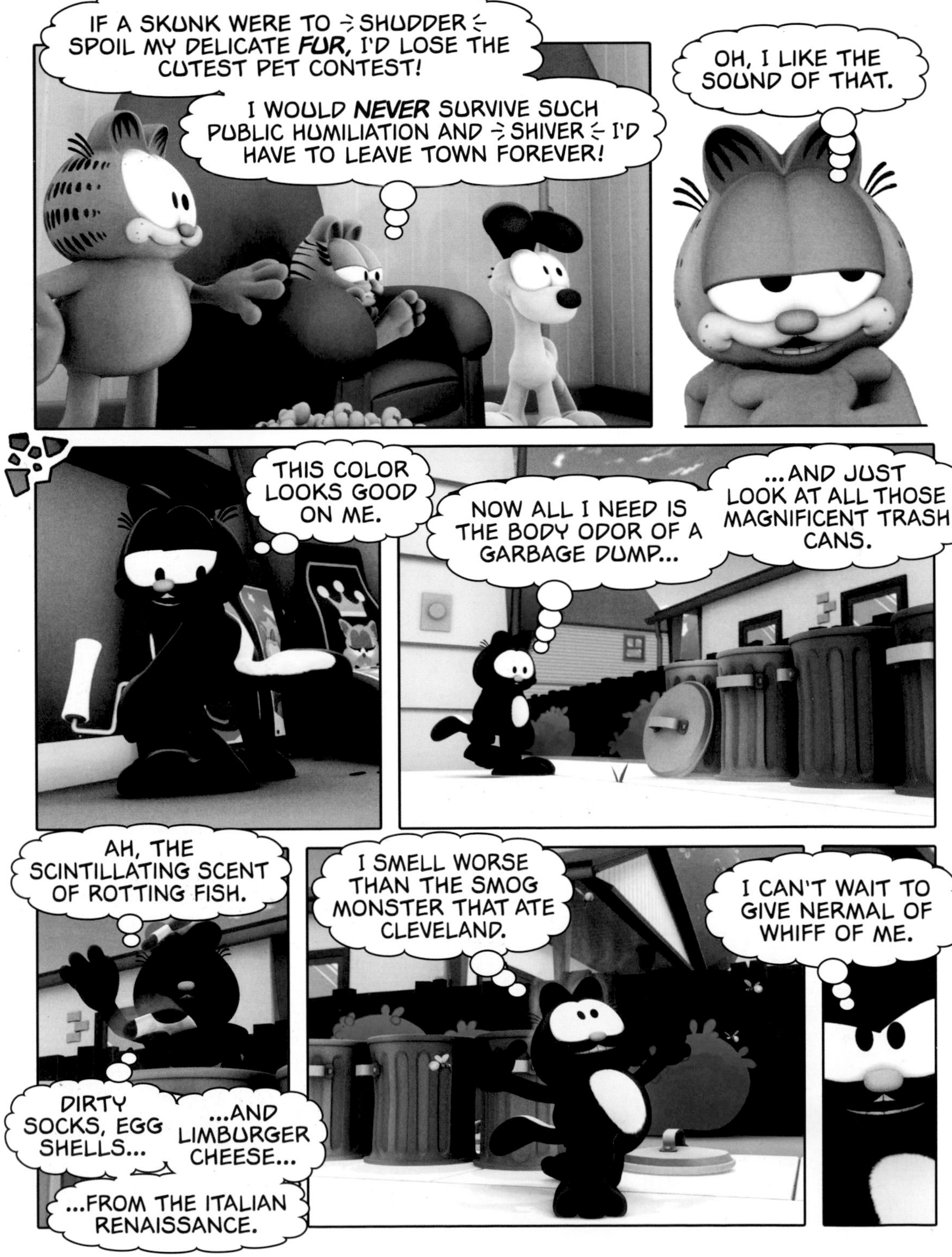
IF A SKUNK WERE TO SHUDDER SPOIL MY DELICATE FUR, I'D LOSE THE CUTEST PET CONTEST!
I WOULD NEVER SURVIVE SUCH PUBLIC HUMILIATION AND SHIVER I'D HAVE TO LEAVE TOWN FOREVER!
OH, I LIKE THE SOUND OF THAT.
THIS COLOR LOOKS GOOD ON ME.
NOW ALL I NEED IS THE BODY ODOR OF A GARBAGE DUMP...
...AND JUST LOOK AT ALL THOSE MAGNIFICENT TRASH CANS.
AH, THE SCINTILLATING SCENT OF ROTTING FISH.
DIRTY SOCKS, EGG SHELLS...
...AND LIMBURGER CHEESE...
...FROM THE ITALIAN RENAISSANCE.
I SMELL WORSE THAN THE SMOG MONSTER THAT ATE CLEVELAND.
I CAN'T WAIT TO GIVE NERMAL OF WHIFF OF ME.

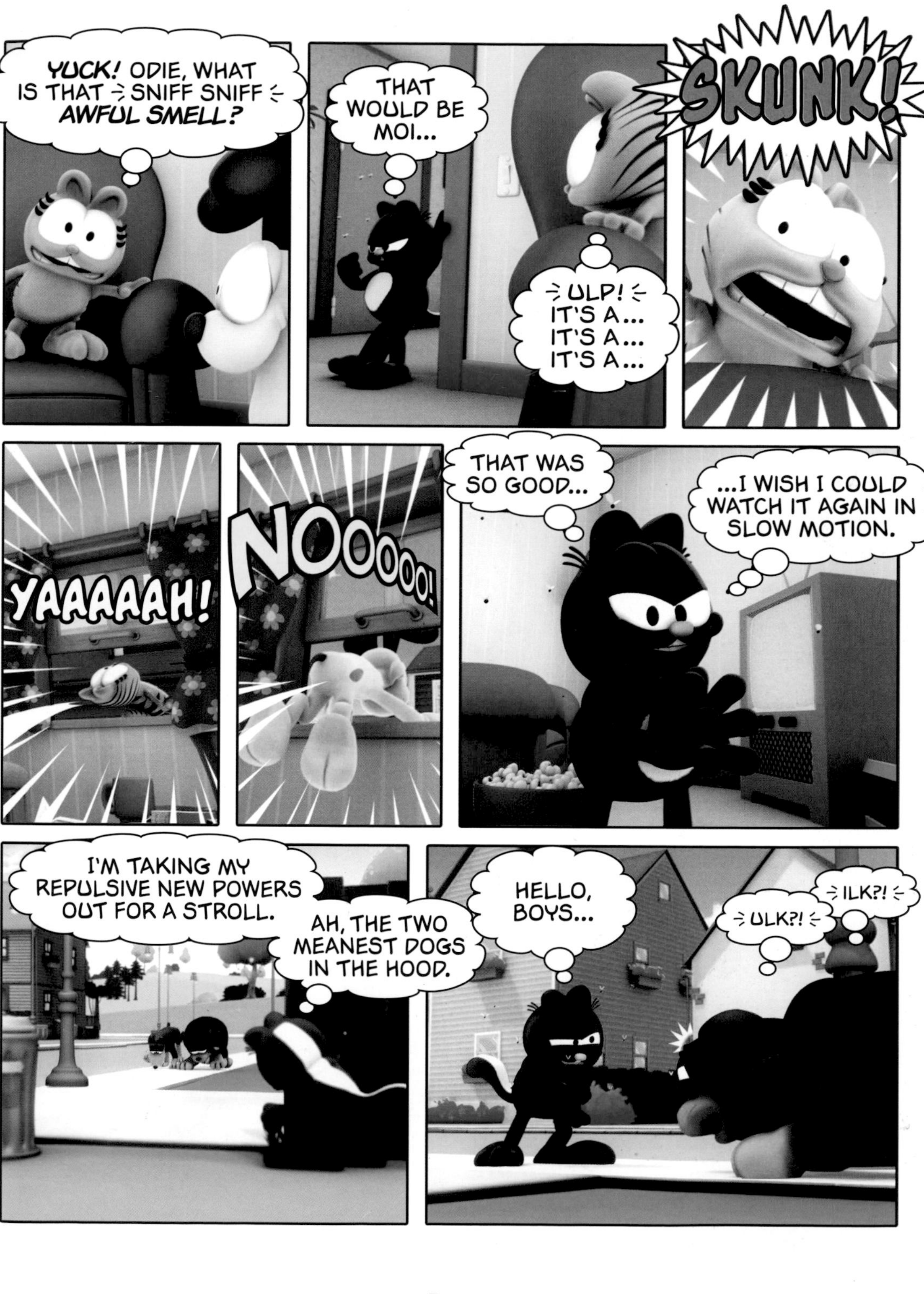
YUCK! ODIE, WHAT IS THAT ⇒ SNIFF SNIFF ⇐ AWFUL SMELL?
THAT WOULD BE MOI...
⇒ ULP! ⇐ IT'S A... IT'S A... IT'S A...
SKUNK!
YAAAAAH!
NOOOOO!
THAT WAS SO GOOD...
...I WISH I COULD WATCH IT AGAIN IN SLOW MOTION.
I'M TAKING MY REPULSIVE NEW POWERS OUT FOR A STROLL.
AH, THE TWO MEANEST DOGS IN THE HOOD.
HELLO, BOYS...
⇒ ULK?! ⇐
⇒ ILK?! ⇐

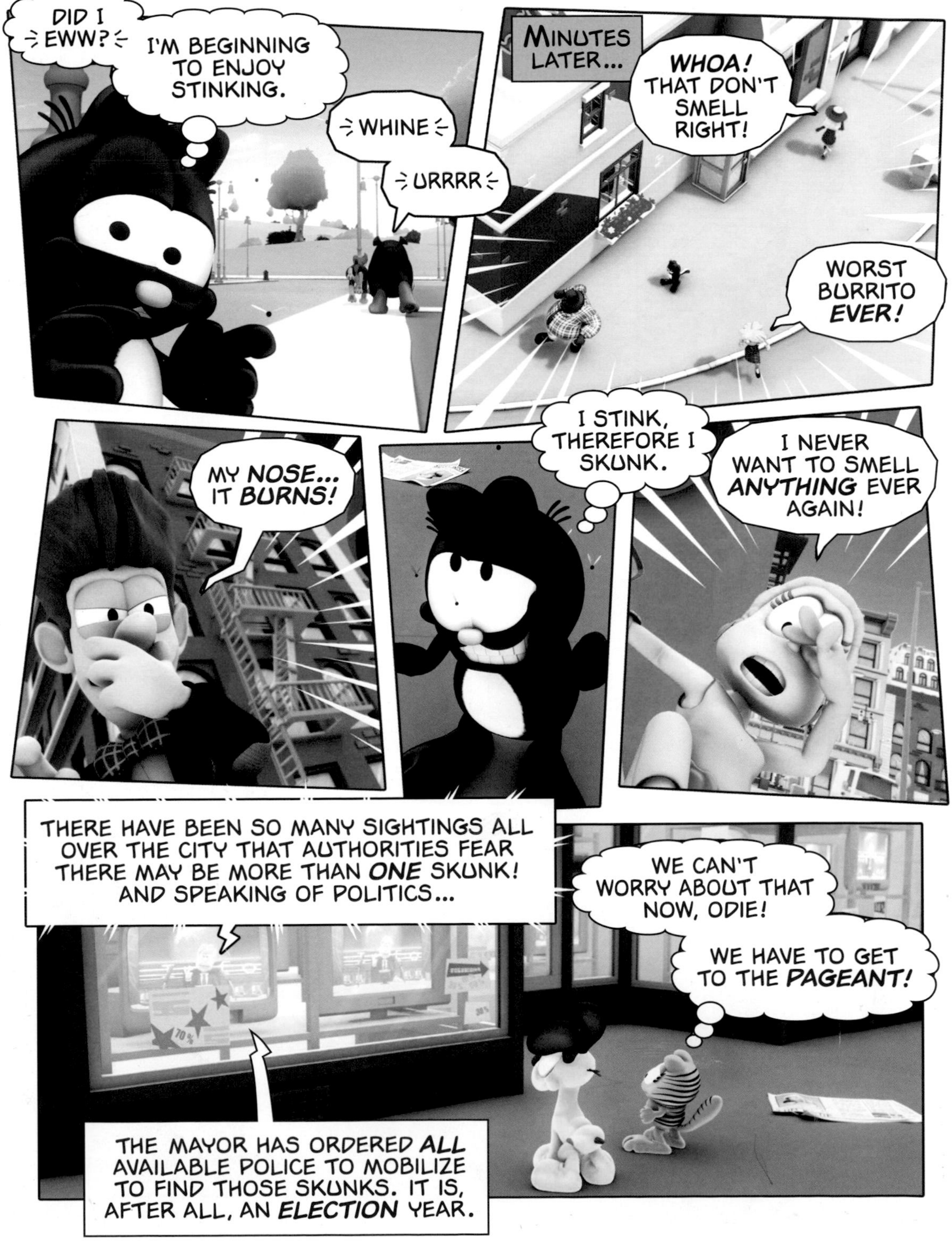
DID I EWW?
I'M BEGINNING TO ENJOY STINKING.
WHINE
URRRR
MINUTES LATER...
WHOA! THAT DON'T SMELL RIGHT!
WORST BURRITO EVER!
MY NOSE... IT BURNS!
I STINK, THEREFORE I SKUNK.
I NEVER WANT TO SMELL ANYTHING EVER AGAIN!
THERE HAVE BEEN SO MANY SIGHTINGS ALL OVER THE CITY THAT AUTHORITIES FEAR THERE MAY BE MORE THAN ONE SKUNK! AND SPEAKING OF POLITICS...
WE CAN'T WORRY ABOUT THAT NOW, ODIE!
WE HAVE TO GET TO THE PAGEANT!
THE MAYOR HAS ORDERED ALL AVAILABLE POLICE TO MOBILIZE TO FIND THOSE SKUNKS. IT IS, AFTER ALL, AN ELECTION YEAR.

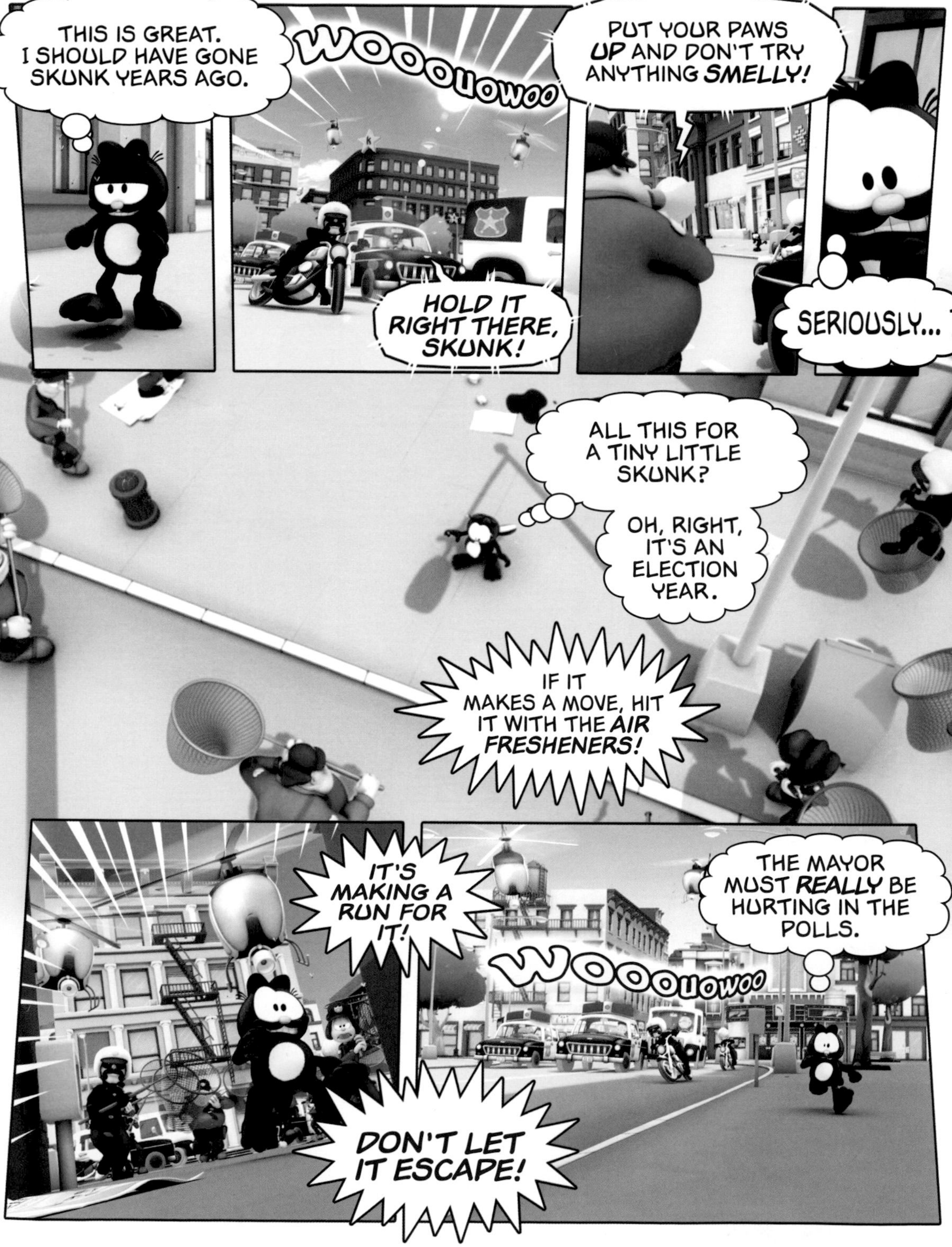

THIS IS GREAT. I SHOULD HAVE GONE SKUNK YEARS AGO.
WOOOOUOWOO
HOLD IT RIGHT THERE, SKUNK!
PUT YOUR PAWS UP AND DON'T TRY ANYTHING SMELLY!
SERIOUSLY...
ALL THIS FOR A TINY LITTLE SKUNK?
OH, RIGHT, IT'S AN ELECTION YEAR.
IF IT MAKES A MOVE, HIT IT WITH THE AIR FRESHENERS!
IT'S MAKING A RUN FOR IT!
DON'T LET IT ESCAPE!
WOOOOUOWOO
THE MAYOR MUST REALLY BE HURTING IN THE POLLS.

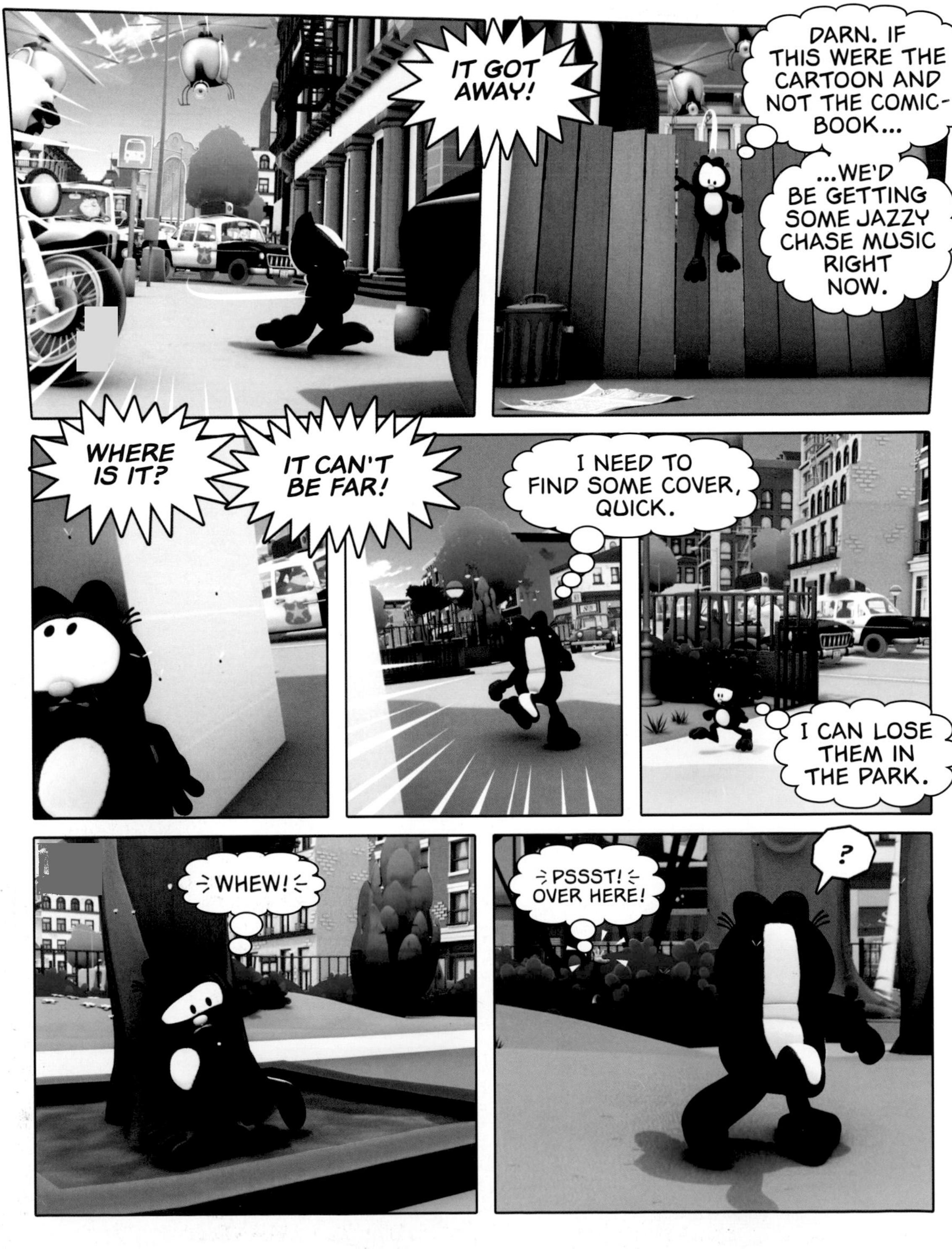
IT GOT AWAY!
DARN. IF THIS WERE THE CARTOON AND NOT THE COMIC-BOOK...
...WE'D BE GETTING SOME JAZZY CHASE MUSIC RIGHT NOW.
WHERE IS IT?
IT CAN'T BE FAR!
I NEED TO FIND SOME COVER, QUICK.
I CAN LOSE THEM IN THE PARK.
WHEW!
PSSST! OVER HERE!
?

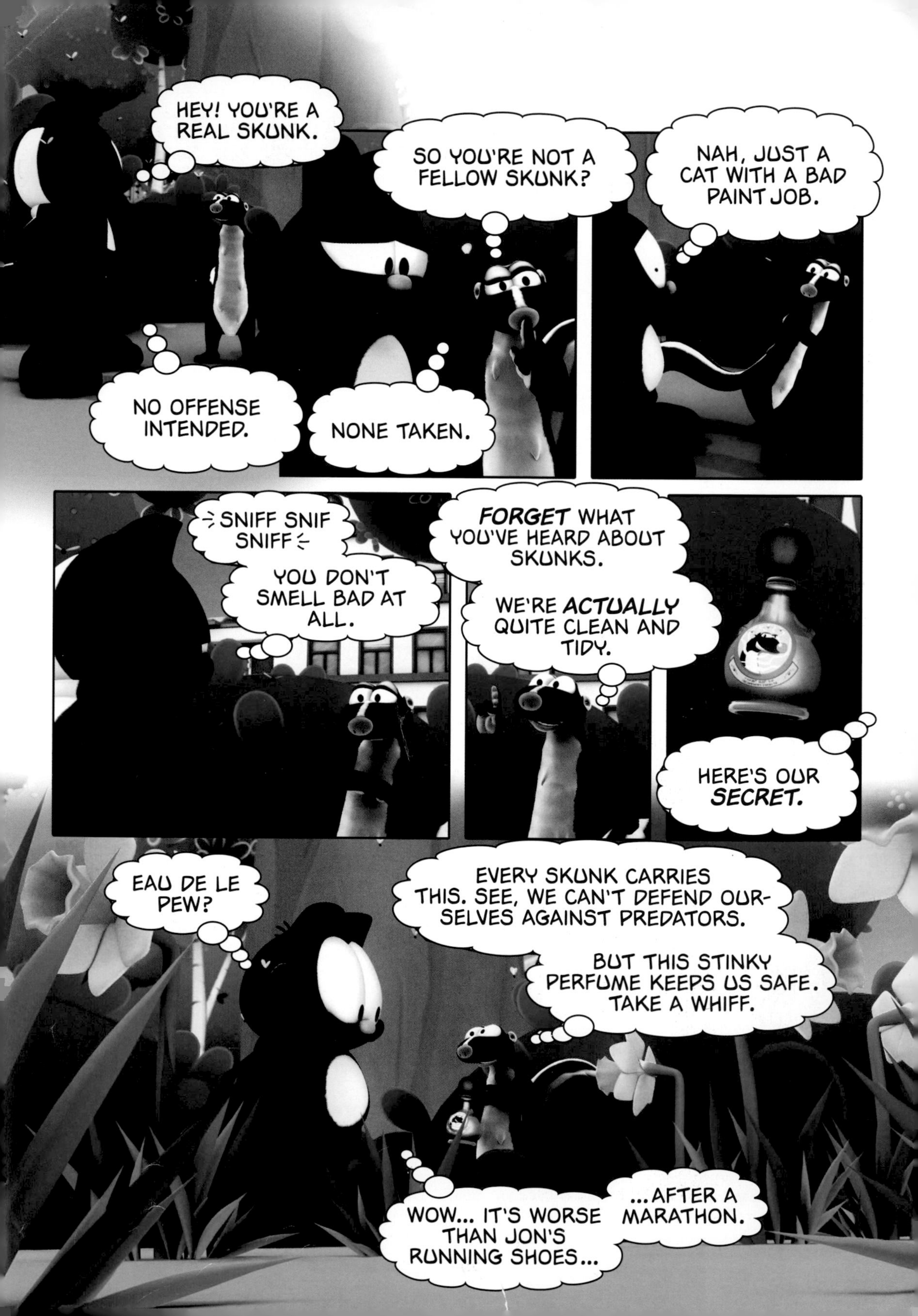
HEY! YOU'RE A REAL SKUNK.
NO OFFENSE INTENDED.
SO YOU'RE NOT A FELLOW SKUNK?
NONE TAKEN.
NAH, JUST A CAT WITH A BAD PAINT JOB.
SNIFF SNIF SNIFF
YOU DON'T SMELL BAD AT ALL.
FORGET WHAT YOU'VE HEARD ABOUT SKUNKS.
WE'RE ACTUALLY QUITE CLEAN AND TIDY.
HERE'S OUR SECRET.
EAU DE LE PEW?
EVERY SKUNK CARRIES THIS. SEE, WE CAN'T DEFEND OURSELVES AGAINST PREDATORS.
BUT THIS STINKY PERFUME KEEPS US SAFE. TAKE A WHIFF.
WOW... IT'S WORSE THAN JON'S RUNNING SHOES...
...AFTER A MARATHON.

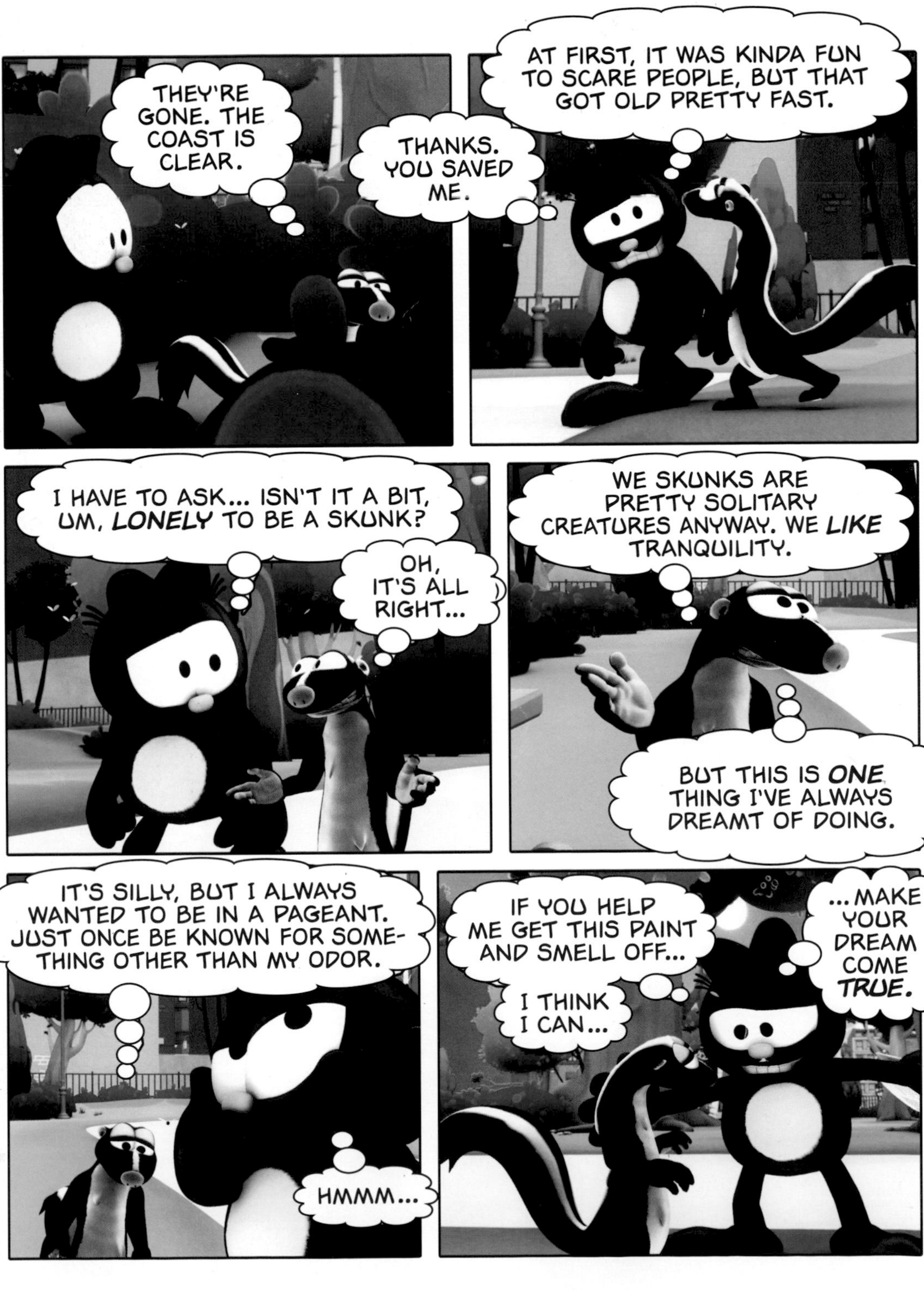
THEY'RE GONE. THE COAST IS CLEAR.
THANKS. YOU SAVED ME.
AT FIRST, IT WAS KINDA FUN TO SCARE PEOPLE, BUT THAT GOT OLD PRETTY FAST.
I HAVE TO ASK... ISN'T IT A BIT, UM, *LONELY* TO BE A SKUNK?
OH, IT'S ALL RIGHT...
WE SKUNKS ARE PRETTY SOLITARY CREATURES ANYWAY. WE *LIKE* TRANQUILITY.
BUT THIS IS *ONE* THING I'VE ALWAYS DREAMT OF DOING.
IT'S SILLY, BUT I ALWAYS WANTED TO BE IN A PAGEANT. JUST ONCE BE KNOWN FOR SOME-THING OTHER THAN MY ODOR.
HMMM...
IF YOU HELP ME GET THIS PAINT AND SMELL OFF...
I THINK I CAN...
...MAKE YOUR DREAM COME *TRUE*.

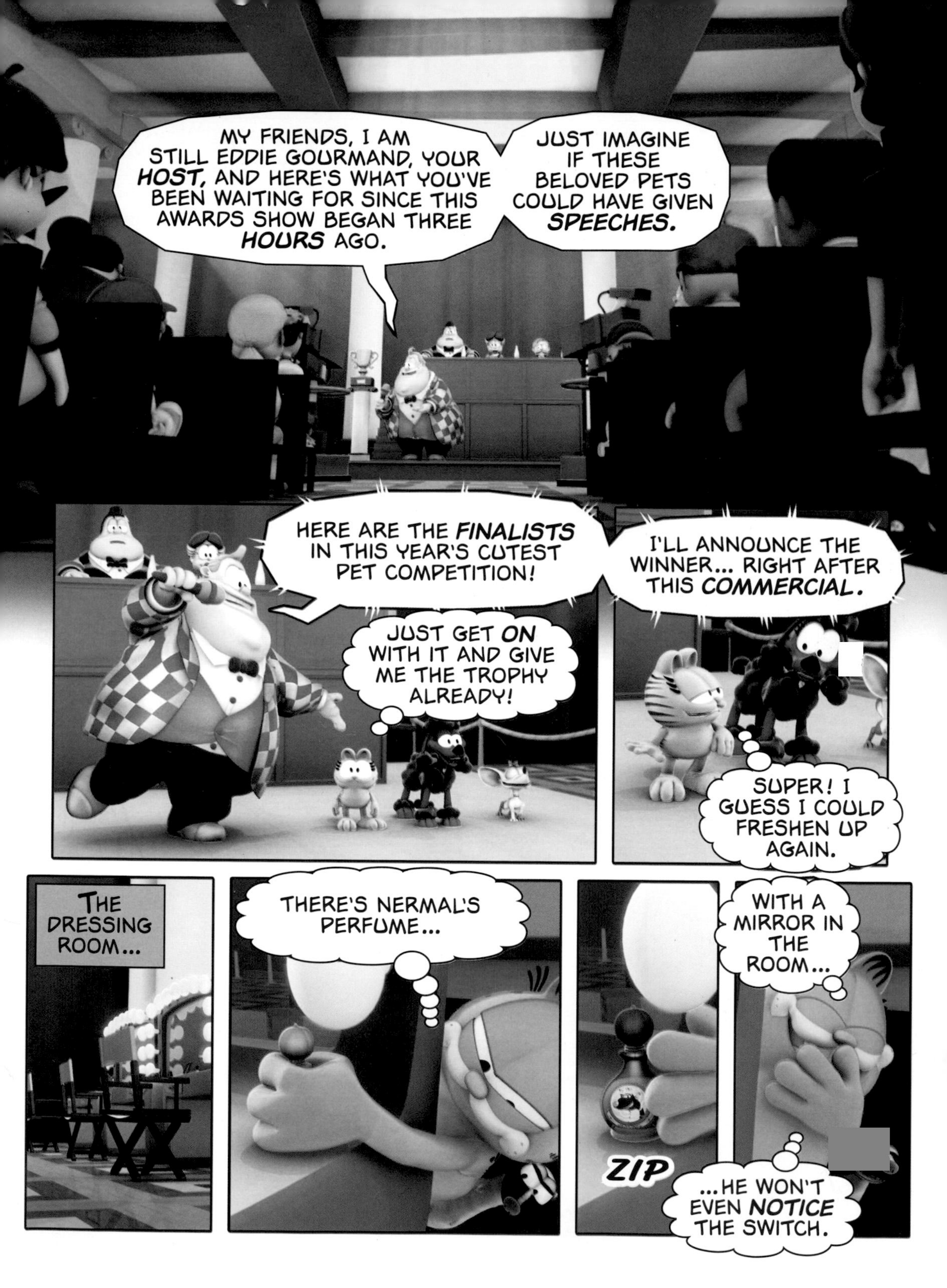
MY FRIENDS, I AM STILL EDDIE GOURMAND, YOUR HOST, AND HERE'S WHAT YOU'VE BEEN WAITING FOR SINCE THIS AWARDS SHOW BEGAN THREE HOURS AGO.
JUST IMAGINE IF THESE BELOVED PETS COULD HAVE GIVEN SPEECHES.
HERE ARE THE FINALISTS IN THIS YEAR'S CUTEST PET COMPETITION!
JUST GET ON WITH IT AND GIVE ME THE TROPHY ALREADY!
I'LL ANNOUNCE THE WINNER... RIGHT AFTER THIS COMMERCIAL.
SUPER! I GUESS I COULD FRESHEN UP AGAIN.
THE DRESSING ROOM...
THERE'S NERMAL'S PERFUME...
ZIP
WITH A MIRROR IN THE ROOM...
...HE WON'T EVEN NOTICE THE SWITCH.

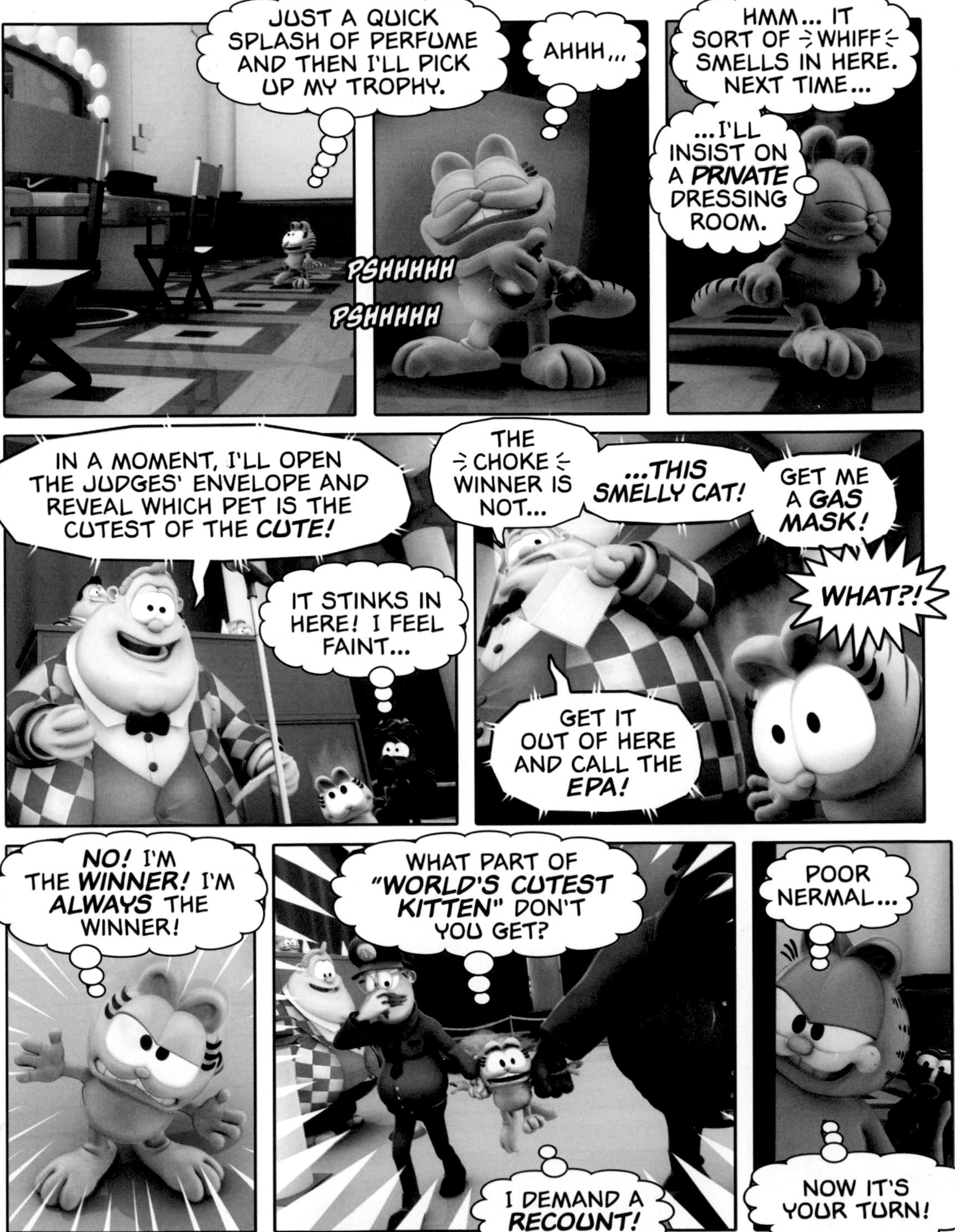
JUST A QUICK SPLASH OF PERFUME AND THEN I'LL PICK UP MY TROPHY.
AHHH...
PSHHHHH
PSHHHHH
HMM... IT SORT OF WHIFF SMELLS IN HERE. NEXT TIME...
...I'LL INSIST ON A PRIVATE DRESSING ROOM.
IN A MOMENT, I'LL OPEN THE JUDGES' ENVELOPE AND REVEAL WHICH PET IS THE CUTEST OF THE CUTE!
IT STINKS IN HERE! I FEEL FAINT...
THE ⇒CHOKE⇐ WINNER IS NOT...
...THIS SMELLY CAT!
GET ME A GAS MASK!
WHAT?!
GET IT OUT OF HERE AND CALL THE EPA!
NO! I'M THE WINNER! I'M ALWAYS THE WINNER!
WHAT PART OF "WORLD'S CUTEST KITTEN" DON'T YOU GET?
I DEMAND A RECOUNT!
POOR NERMAL...
NOW IT'S YOUR TURN!

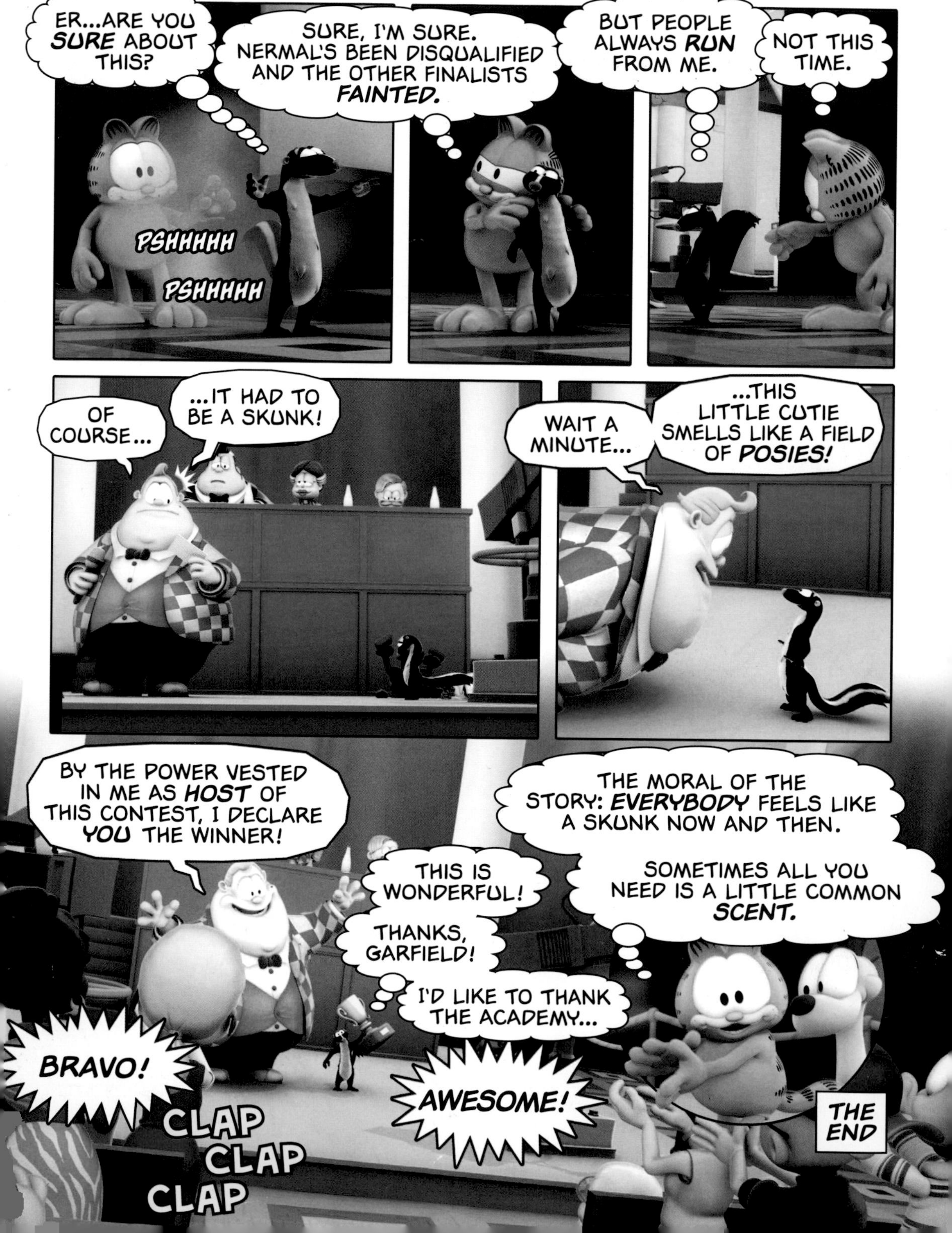

ER...ARE YOU SURE ABOUT THIS?
SURE, I'M SURE. NERMAL'S BEEN DISQUALIFIED AND THE OTHER FINALISTS FAINTED.
PSHHHHH
PSHHHHH
BUT PEOPLE ALWAYS RUN FROM ME.
NOT THIS TIME.
OF COURSE...
...IT HAD TO BE A SKUNK!
WAIT A MINUTE...
...THIS LITTLE CUTIE SMELLS LIKE A FIELD OF POSIES!
BY THE POWER VESTED IN ME AS HOST OF THIS CONTEST, I DECLARE YOU THE WINNER!
THE MORAL OF THE STORY: EVERYBODY FEELS LIKE A SKUNK NOW AND THEN.
THIS IS WONDERFUL!
SOMETIMES ALL YOU NEED IS A LITTLE COMMON SCENT.
THANKS, GARFIELD!
I'D LIKE TO THANK THE ACADEMY...
BRAVO!
AWESOME!
CLAP
CLAP
CLAP
THE END

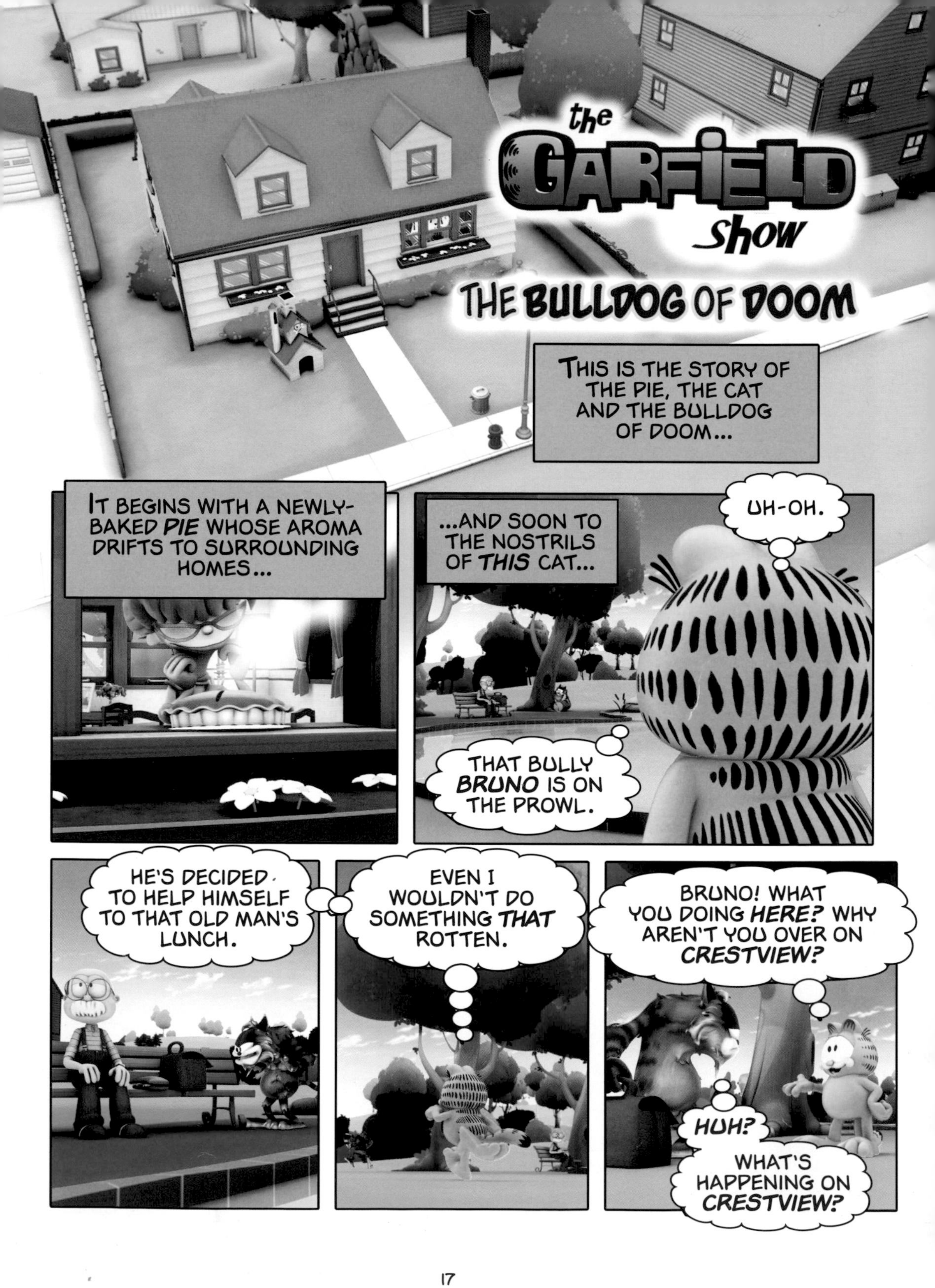
the GARFIELD show
THE BULLDOG OF DOOM
THIS IS THE STORY OF THE PIE, THE CAT AND THE BULLDOG OF DOOM...
IT BEGINS WITH A NEWLY-BAKED PIE WHOSE AROMA DRIFTS TO SURROUNDING HOMES...
...AND SOON TO THE NOSTRILS OF THIS CAT...
UH-OH.
THAT BULLY BRUNO IS ON THE PROWL.
HE'S DECIDED TO HELP HIMSELF TO THAT OLD MAN'S LUNCH.
EVEN I WOULDN'T DO SOMETHING THAT ROTTEN.
BRUNO! WHAT YOU DOING HERE? WHY AREN'T YOU OVER ON CRESTVIEW?
HUH?
WHAT'S HAPPENING ON CRESTVIEW?

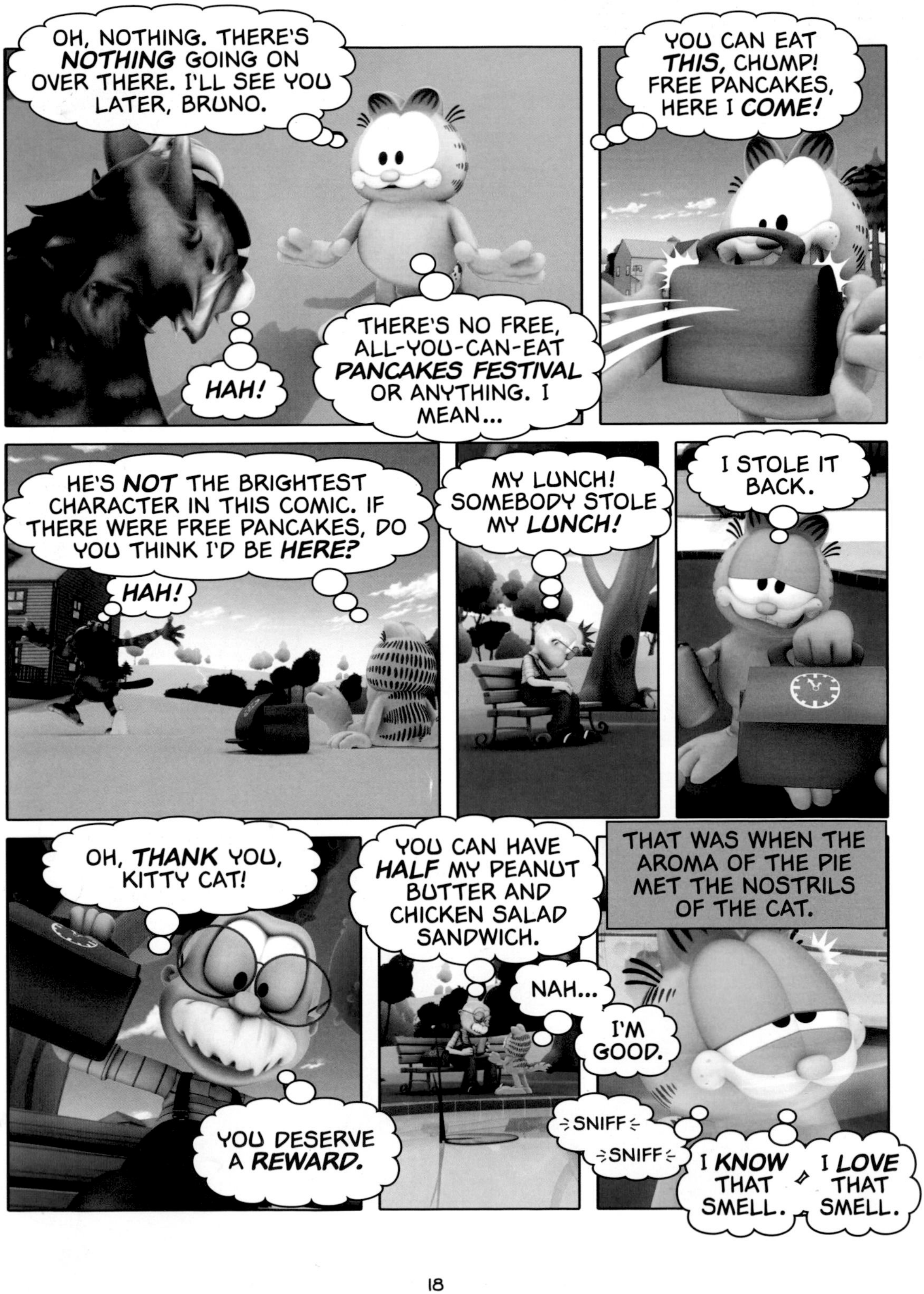
OH, NOTHING. THERE'S NOTHING GOING ON OVER THERE. I'LL SEE YOU LATER, BRUNO.
HAH!
THERE'S NO FREE, ALL-YOU-CAN-EAT PANCAKES FESTIVAL OR ANYTHING. I MEAN...
YOU CAN EAT THIS, CHUMP! FREE PANCAKES, HERE I COME!
HE'S NOT THE BRIGHTEST CHARACTER IN THIS COMIC. IF THERE WERE FREE PANCAKES, DO YOU THINK I'D BE HERE?
HAH!
MY LUNCH! SOMEBODY STOLE MY LUNCH!
I STOLE IT BACK.
OH, THANK YOU, KITTY CAT!
YOU DESERVE A REWARD.
YOU CAN HAVE HALF MY PEANUT BUTTER AND CHICKEN SALAD SANDWICH.
NAH...
I'M GOOD.
THAT WAS WHEN THE AROMA OF THE PIE MET THE NOSTRILS OF THE CAT.
SNIFF
SNIFF
I KNOW THAT SMELL.
I LOVE THAT SMELL.

THE AROMA SPOKE TO THE CAT AND IT SAID "DON'T I SMELL DELICIOUS?"

I THINK I LOVE YOU, PIE.

THEN AGAIN, I LOVE ALL PIES.

EXCEPT FOR *RAISIN* PIES.

THOSE TASTE LIKE SOGGY GRAVEL.

UNFORTUNATELY, THE WONDROUS PIE WAS NOT *ALONE*...

OH, NO. IT'S HIM...

...THE *BULLDOG OF DOOM!*

GRRRR

THE PIE AND I CAN NEVER BE...

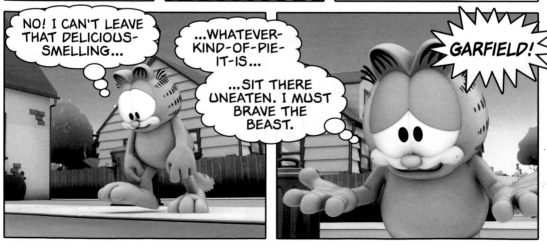

NO! I CAN'T LEAVE THAT DELICIOUS-SMELLING...

...WHATEVER-KIND-OF-PIE-IT-IS...

...SIT THERE UNEATEN. I MUST BRAVE THE BEAST.

GARFIELD!

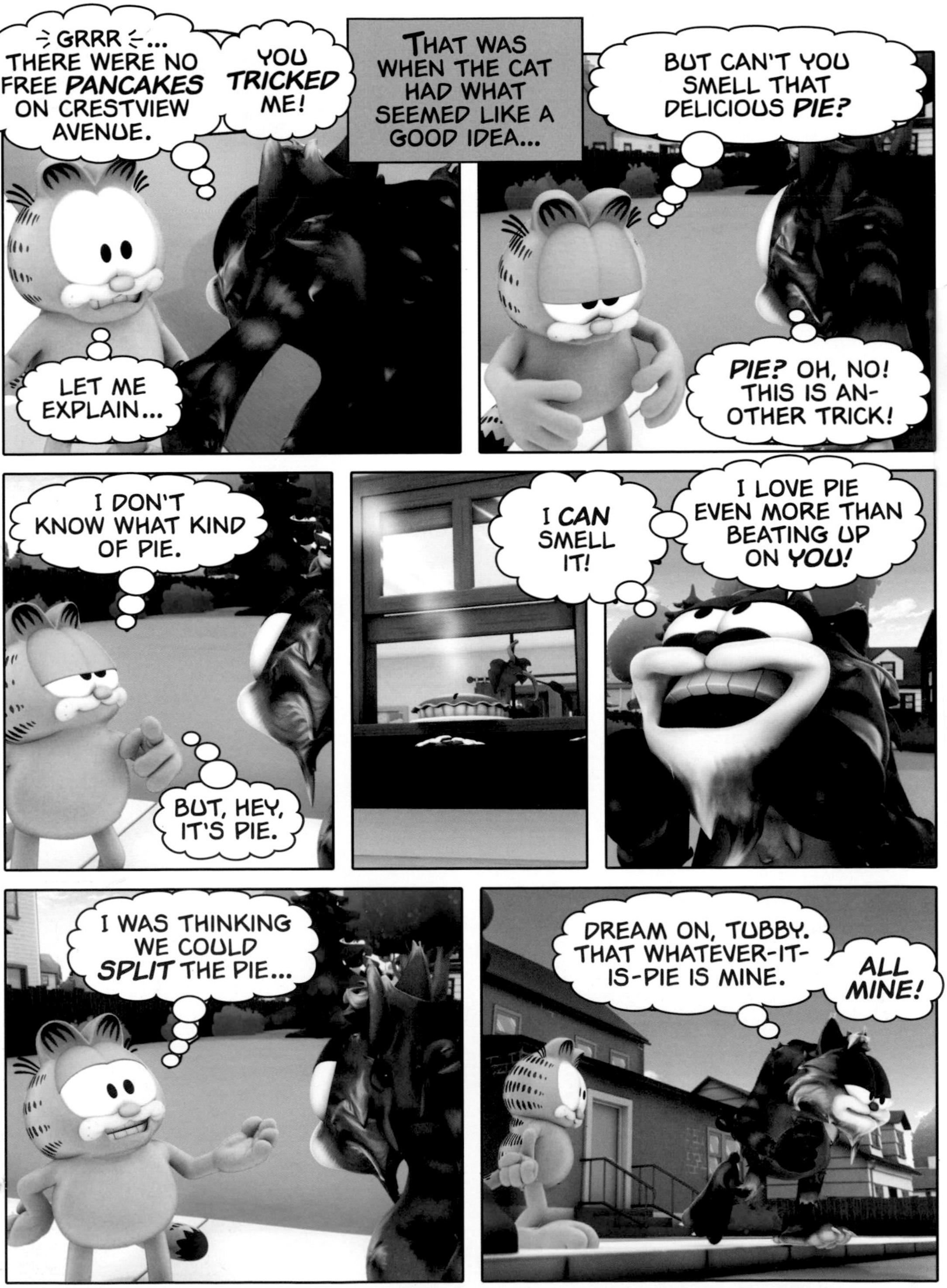

GRRR... THERE WERE NO FREE PANCAKES ON CRESTVIEW AVENUE.
YOU TRICKED ME!
LET ME EXPLAIN...
THAT WAS WHEN THE CAT HAD WHAT SEEMED LIKE A GOOD IDEA...
BUT CAN'T YOU SMELL THAT DELICIOUS PIE?
PIE? OH, NO! THIS IS AN-OTHER TRICK!
I DON'T KNOW WHAT KIND OF PIE.
BUT, HEY, IT'S PIE.
I CAN SMELL IT!
I LOVE PIE EVEN MORE THAN BEATING UP ON YOU!
I WAS THINKING WE COULD SPLIT THE PIE...
DREAM ON, TUBBY. THAT WHATEVER-IT-IS-PIE IS MINE.
ALL MINE!

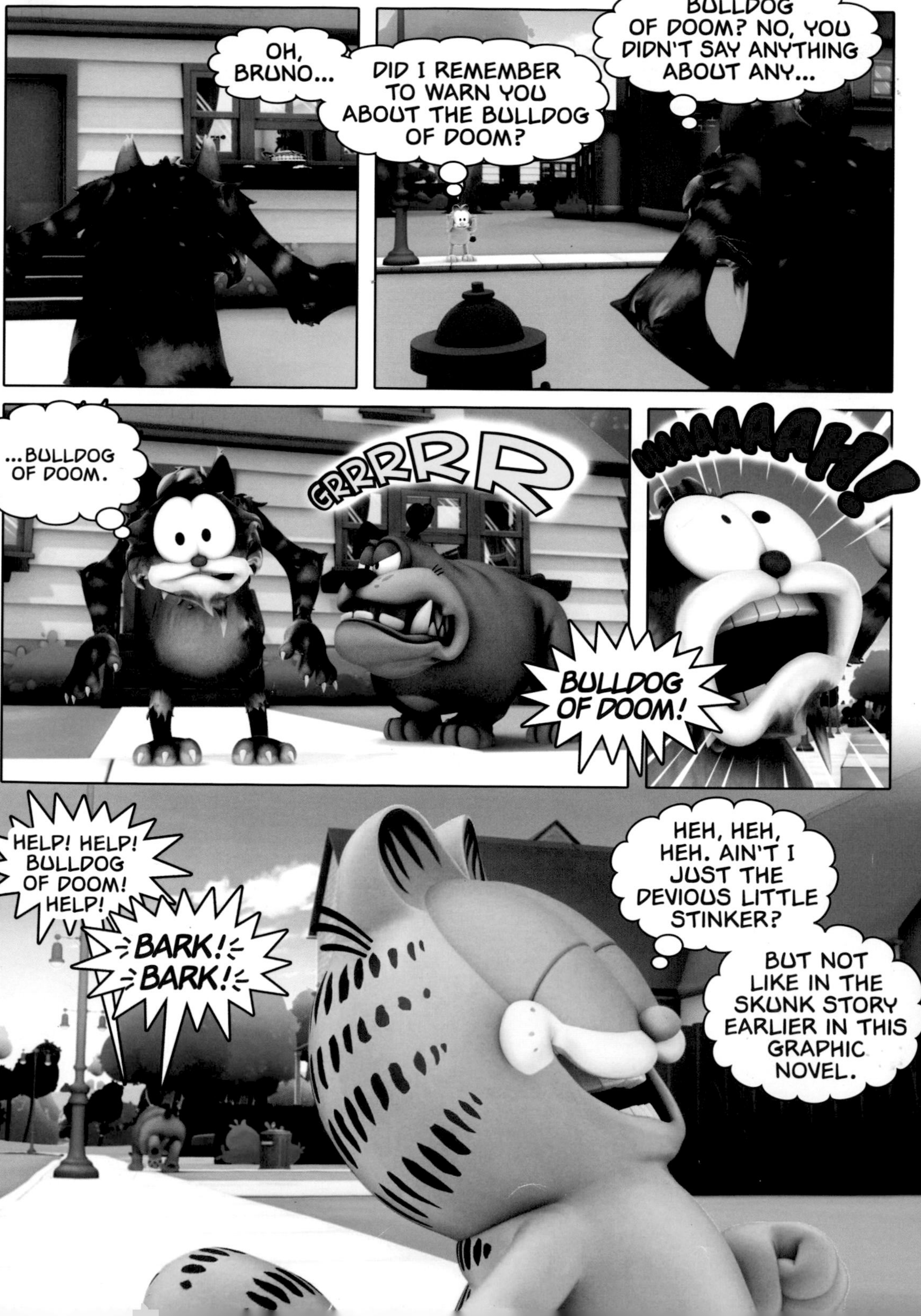
OH, BRUNO...
DID I REMEMBER TO WARN YOU ABOUT THE BULLDOG OF DOOM?
BULLDOG OF DOOM? NO, YOU DIDN'T SAY ANYTHING ABOUT ANY...
...BULLDOG OF DOOM.
GRRRRR
BULLDOG OF DOOM!
HELP! HELP! BULLDOG OF DOOM! HELP!
BARK! BARK!
HEH, HEH, HEH. AIN'T I JUST THE DEVIOUS LITTLE STINKER?
BUT NOT LIKE IN THE SKUNK STORY EARLIER IN THIS GRAPHIC NOVEL.

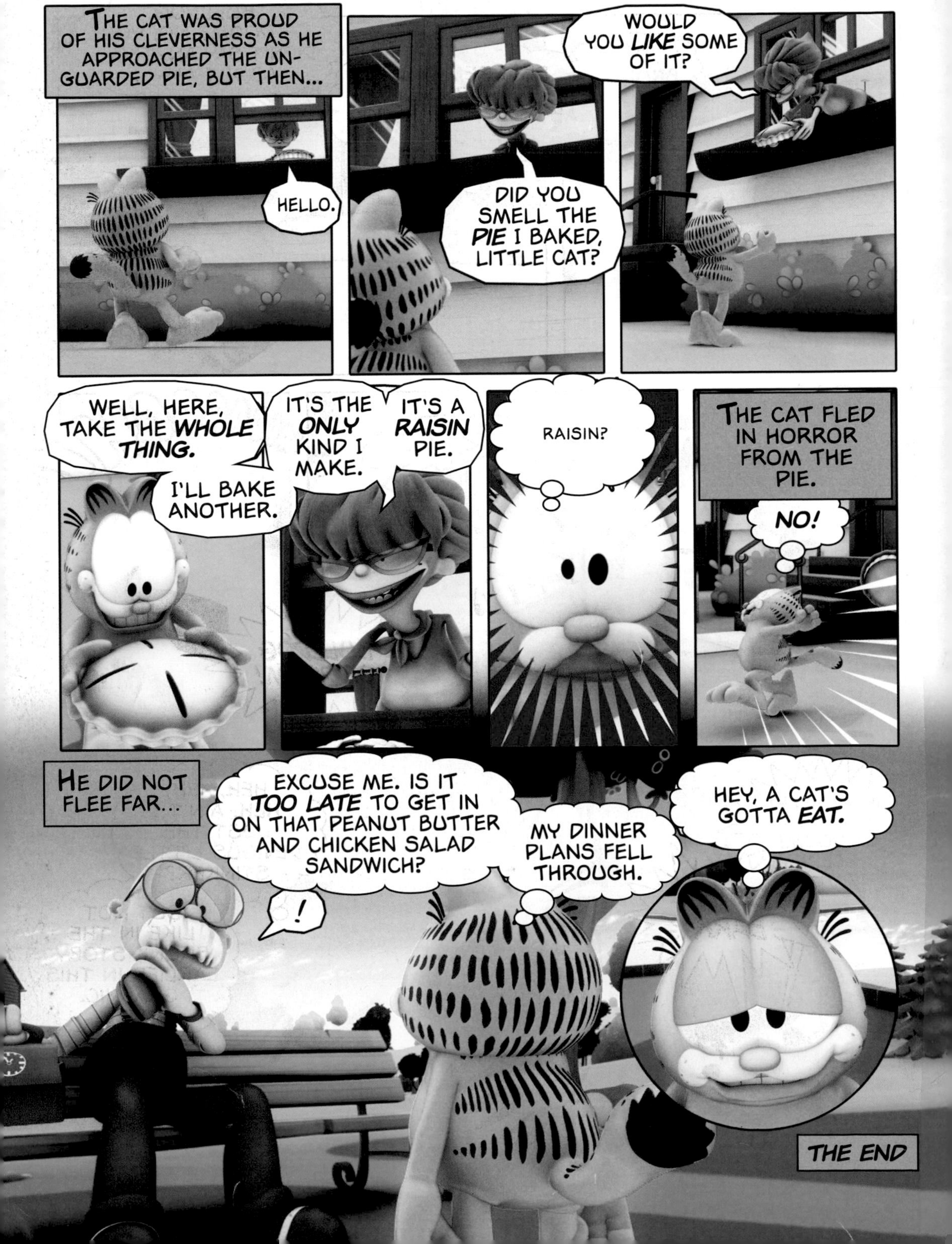
THE CAT WAS PROUD OF HIS CLEVERNESS AS HE APPROACHED THE UN-GUARDED PIE, BUT THEN...
HELLO.
DID YOU SMELL THE PIE I BAKED, LITTLE CAT?
WOULD YOU LIKE SOME OF IT?
WELL, HERE, TAKE THE WHOLE THING.
I'LL BAKE ANOTHER.
IT'S THE ONLY KIND I MAKE.
IT'S A RAISIN PIE.
RAISIN?
THE CAT FLED IN HORROR FROM THE PIE.
NO!
HE DID NOT FLEE FAR...
EXCUSE ME. IS IT TOO LATE TO GET IN ON THAT PEANUT BUTTER AND CHICKEN SALAD SANDWICH?
!
MY DINNER PLANS FELL THROUGH.
HEY, A CAT'S GOTTA EAT.
THE END

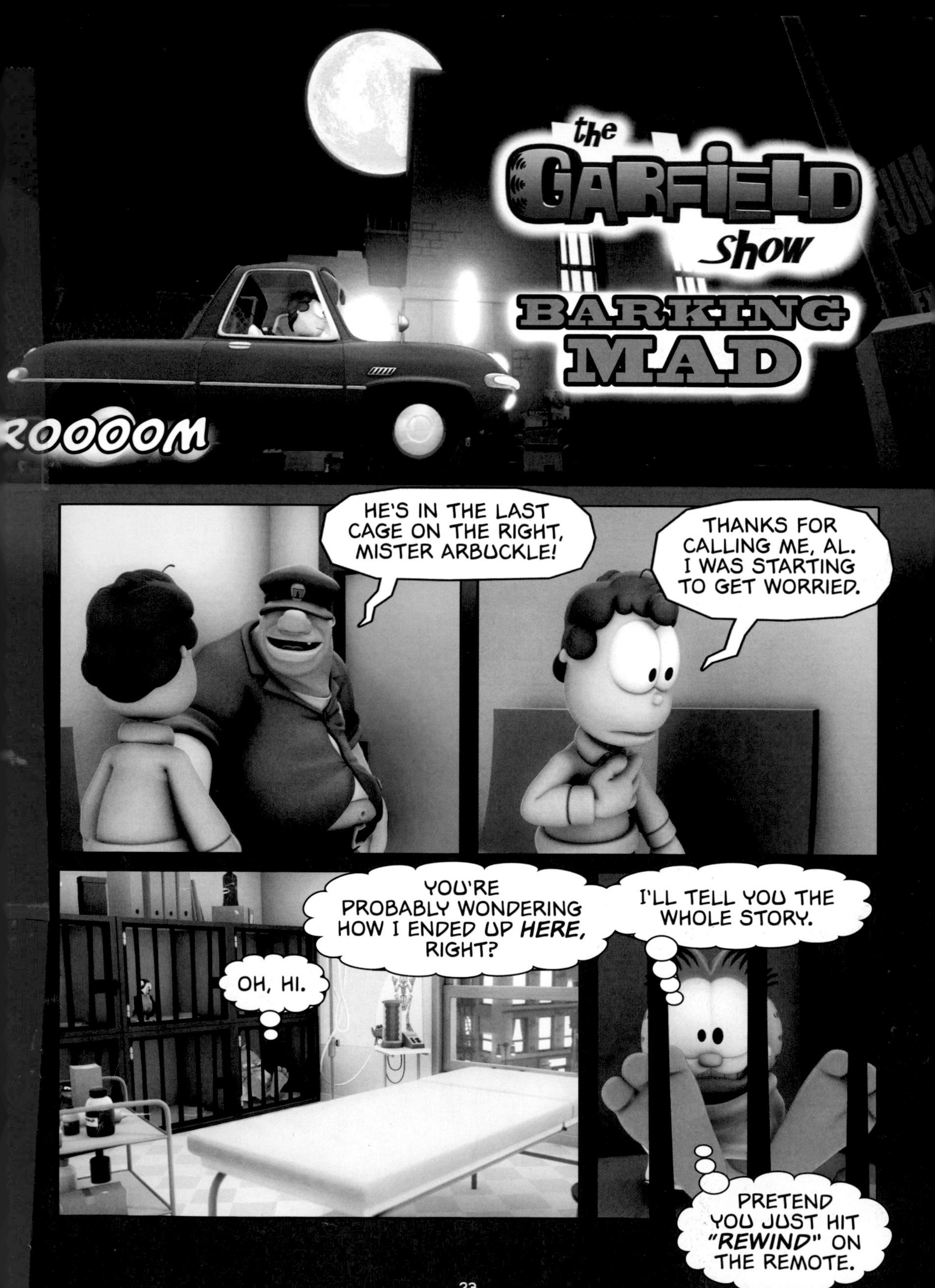
the GARFIELD show
BARKING MAD
ROOOOM
HE'S IN THE LAST CAGE ON THE RIGHT, MISTER ARBUCKLE!
THANKS FOR CALLING ME, AL. I WAS STARTING TO GET WORRIED.
OH, HI.
YOU'RE PROBABLY WONDERING HOW I ENDED UP *HERE,* RIGHT?
I'LL TELL YOU THE WHOLE STORY.
PRETEND YOU JUST HIT *"REWIND"* ON THE REMOTE.

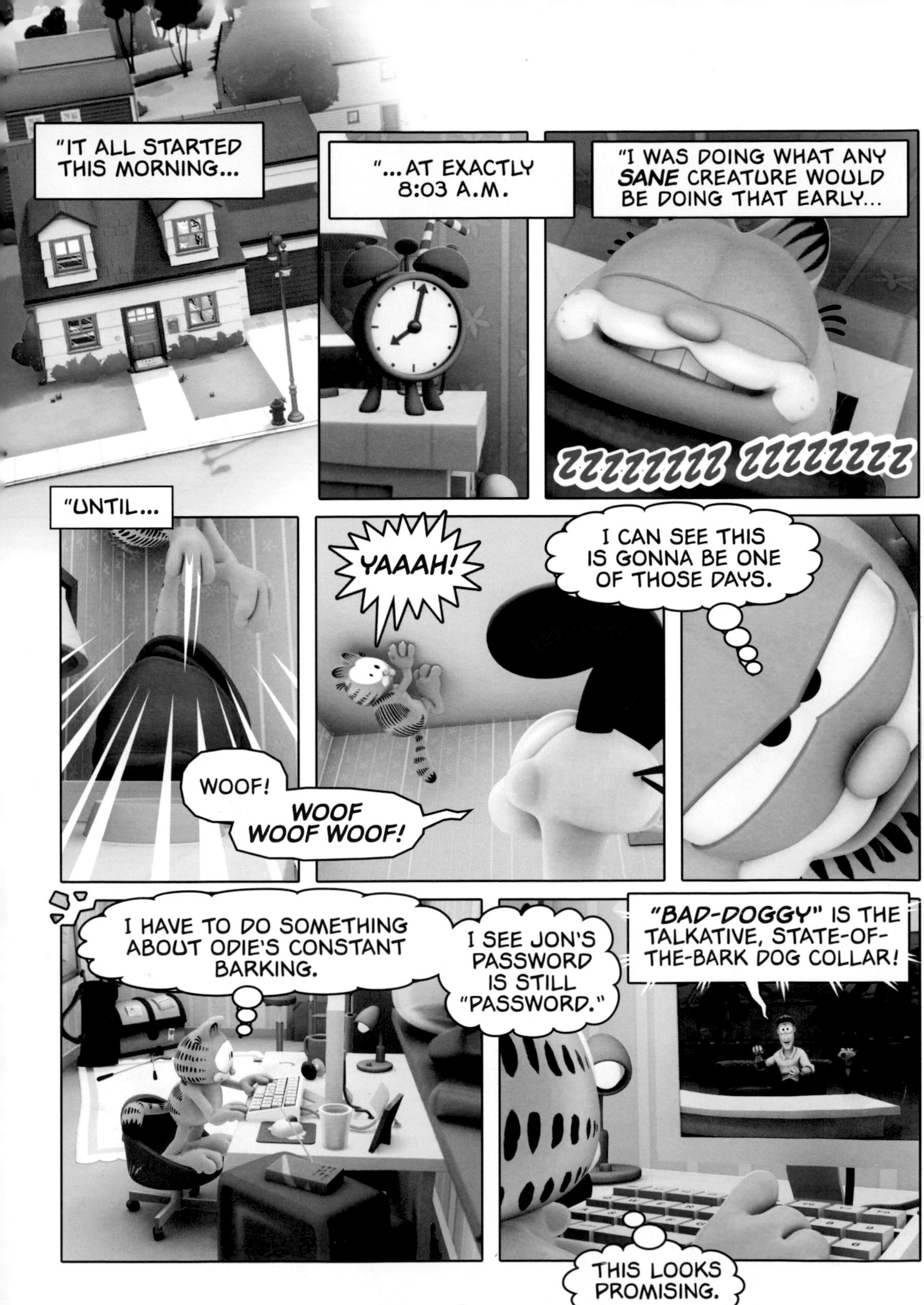
"IT ALL STARTED THIS MORNING...
"...AT EXACTLY 8:03 A.M.
"I WAS DOING WHAT ANY *SANE* CREATURE WOULD BE DOING THAT EARLY...
ZZZZZZZZ ZZZZZZZZ
"UNTIL...
WOOF!
WOOF WOOF WOOF!
YAAAH!
I CAN SEE THIS IS GONNA BE ONE OF THOSE DAYS.
I HAVE TO DO SOMETHING ABOUT ODIE'S CONSTANT BARKING.
I SEE JON'S PASSWORD IS STILL "PASSWORD."
"BAD-DOGGY" IS THE TALKATIVE, STATE-OF-THE-BARK DOG COLLAR!
THIS LOOKS PROMISING.

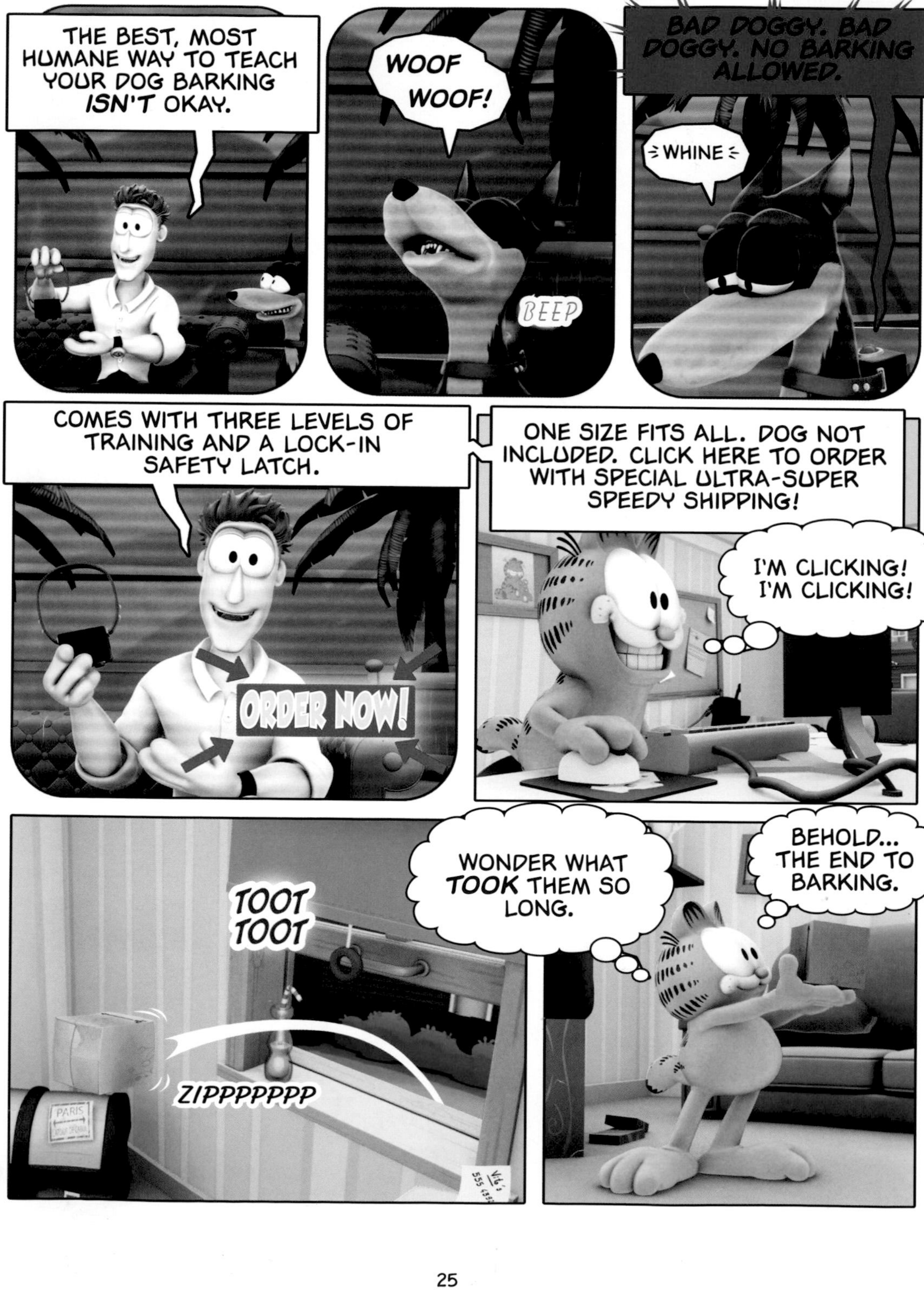

THE BEST, MOST HUMANE WAY TO TEACH YOUR DOG BARKING *ISN'T* OKAY.
WOOF WOOF!
BEEP
BAD DOGGY. BAD DOGGY. NO BARKING ALLOWED.
WHINE
COMES WITH THREE LEVELS OF TRAINING AND A LOCK-IN SAFETY LATCH.
ORDER NOW!
ONE SIZE FITS ALL. DOG NOT INCLUDED. CLICK HERE TO ORDER WITH SPECIAL ULTRA-SUPER SPEEDY SHIPPING!
I'M CLICKING! I'M CLICKING!
TOOT TOOT
ZIPPPPPPPP
WONDER WHAT *TOOK* THEM SO LONG.
BEHOLD... THE END TO BARKING.

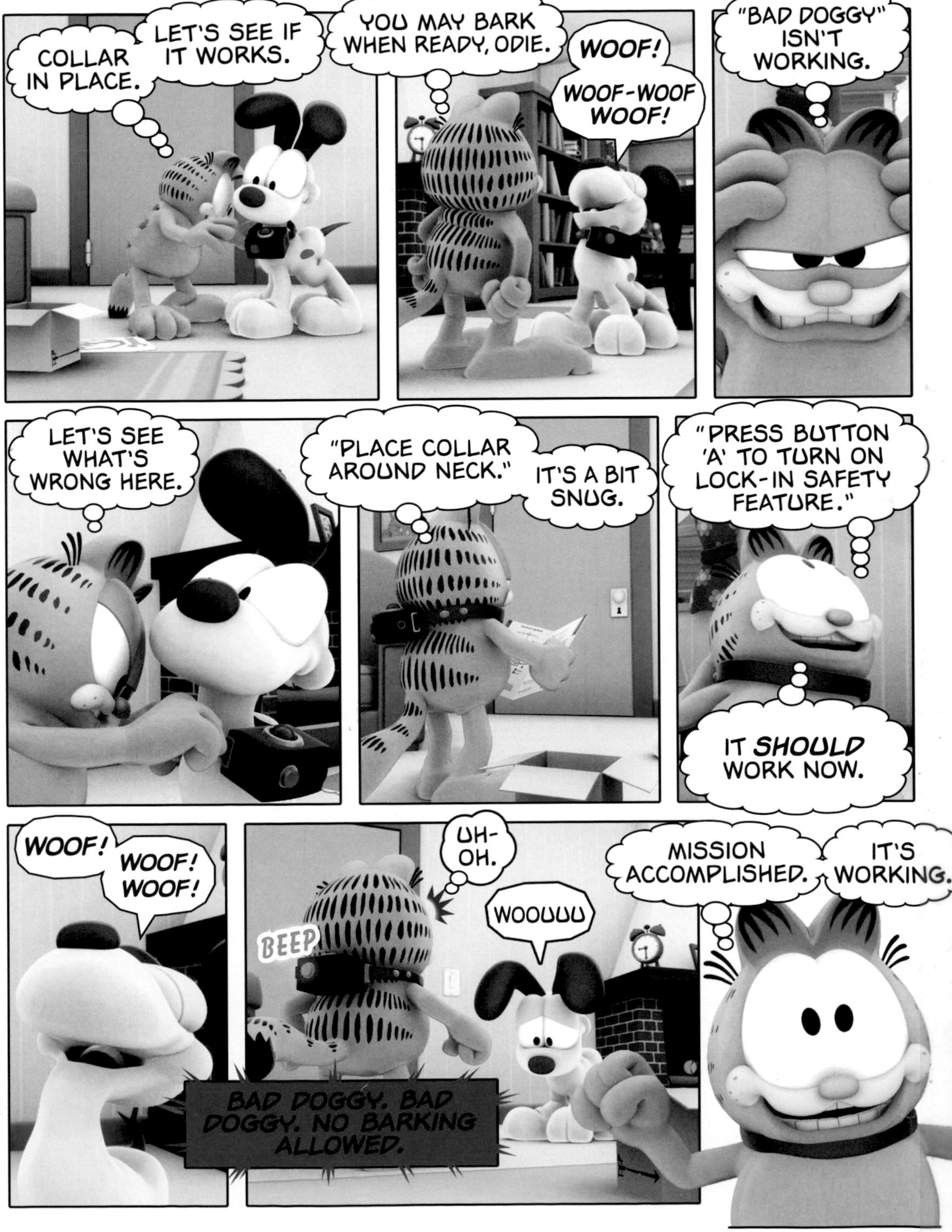
COLLAR IN PLACE.
LET'S SEE IF IT WORKS.
YOU MAY BARK WHEN READY, ODIE.
WOOF!
WOOF-WOOF WOOF!
"BAD DOGGY" ISN'T WORKING.
LET'S SEE WHAT'S WRONG HERE.
"PLACE COLLAR AROUND NECK."
IT'S A BIT SNUG.
"PRESS BUTTON 'A' TO TURN ON LOCK-IN SAFETY FEATURE."
IT SHOULD WORK NOW.
WOOF!
WOOF! WOOF!
BEEP
UH-OH.
WOOUUU
BAD DOGGY. BAD DOGGY. NO BARKING ALLOWED.
MISSION ACCOMPLISHED.
IT'S WORKING.

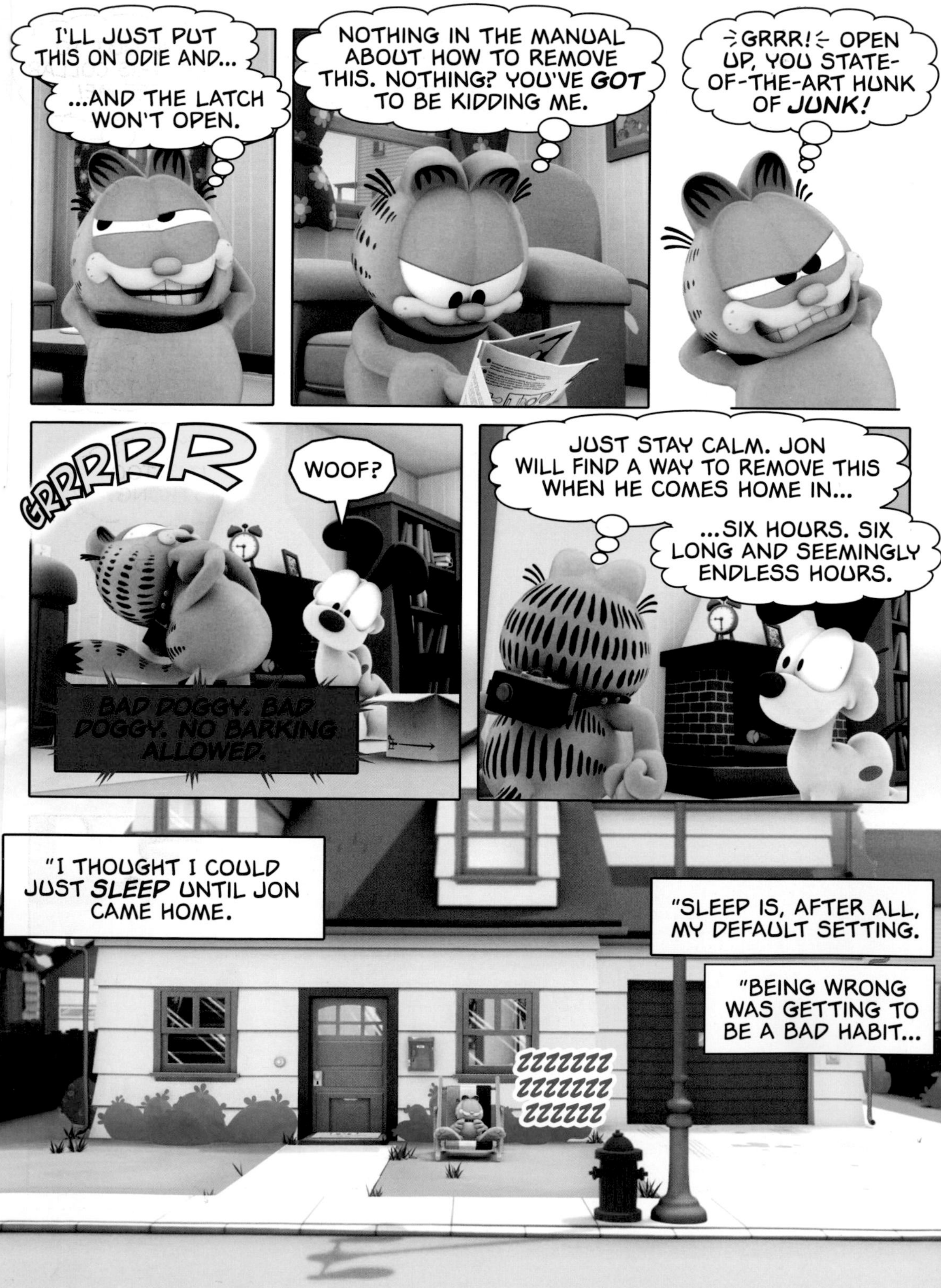

I'LL JUST PUT THIS ON ODIE AND...
...AND THE LATCH WON'T OPEN.
NOTHING IN THE MANUAL ABOUT HOW TO REMOVE THIS. NOTHING? YOU'VE GOT TO BE KIDDING ME.
GRRR! OPEN UP, YOU STATE-OF-THE-ART HUNK OF JUNK!
GRRRRR
WOOF?
BAD DOGGY. BAD DOGGY. NO BARKING ALLOWED.
JUST STAY CALM. JON WILL FIND A WAY TO REMOVE THIS WHEN HE COMES HOME IN...
...SIX HOURS. SIX LONG AND SEEMINGLY ENDLESS HOURS.
"I THOUGHT I COULD JUST SLEEP UNTIL JON CAME HOME.
"SLEEP IS, AFTER ALL, MY DEFAULT SETTING.
"BEING WRONG WAS GETTING TO BE A BAD HABIT...
ZZZZZZZ ZZZZZZZ ZZZZZZ

WOOF!

WOOF!

BEEP BEEP BEEP

WOOF!

BAD DOGGY. BAD DOGGY. NO BARKING ALLOWED.

GRIND

BAD DOGGY! DIDN'T YOU HEAR ME?

NO BARKING ALLOWED!

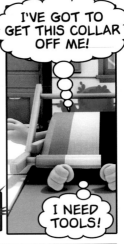

I'VE GOT TO GET THIS COLLAR OFF ME!

I NEED TOOLS!

THERE ARE *TOO* MANY DOGS IN THIS NEIGHBORHOOD.

I *CAN'T* WAIT UNTIL JON GETS HOME.

GNN!

ARRGH! IT'S NO USE.

IT'S TOO STRONG.

CONGRATULATIONS. YOU HAVE SUCCESSFULLY ACTIVATED *LEVEL TWO* OF THE REINFORCE- MENT TRAINING SOFTWARE.

LEVEL *TWO?* THIS CAN'T *POSSIBLY* BE GOOD.

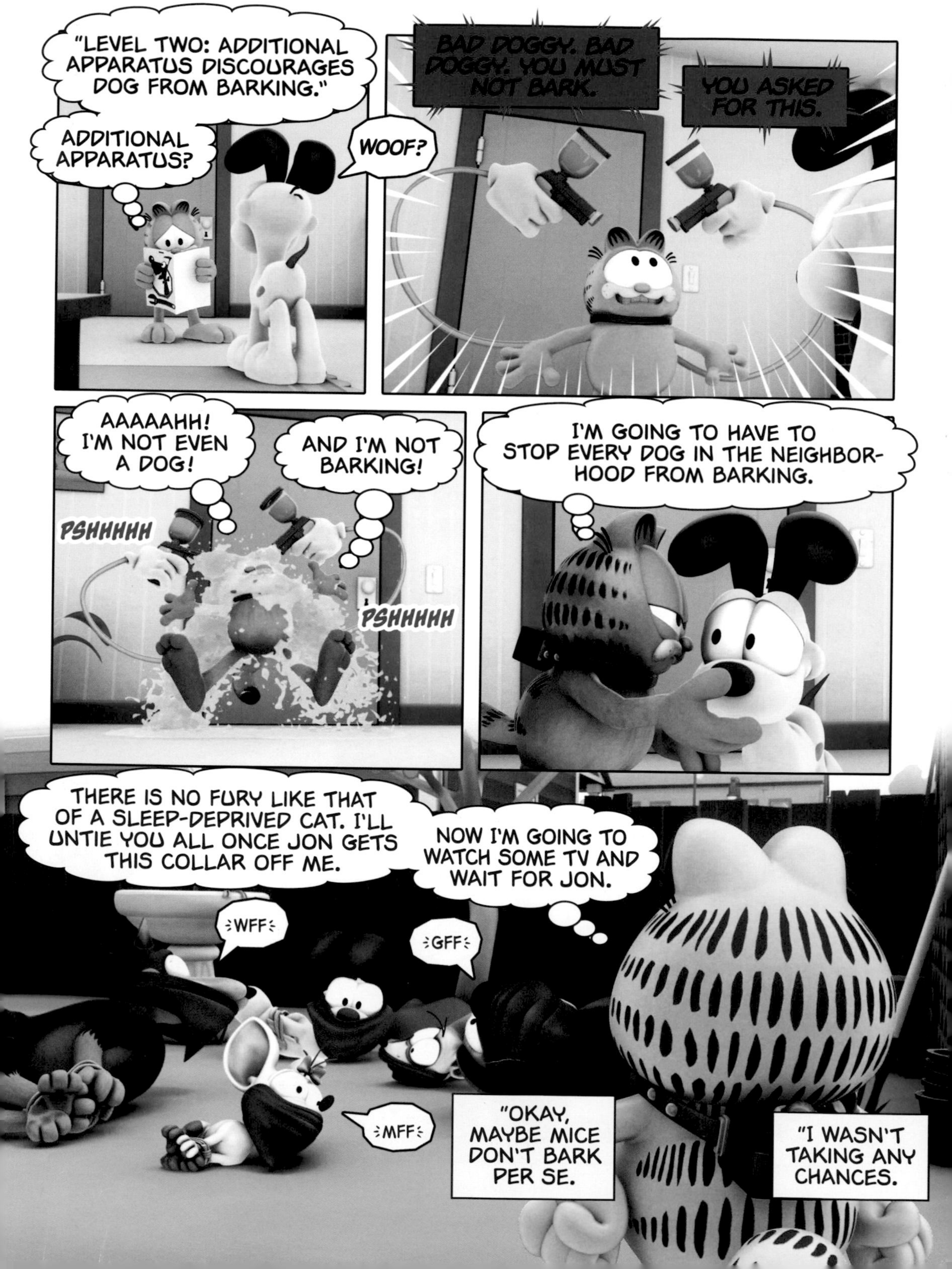
"LEVEL TWO: ADDITIONAL APPARATUS DISCOURAGES DOG FROM BARKING."
ADDITIONAL APPARATUS?
WOOF?
BAD DOGGY. BAD DOGGY. YOU MUST NOT BARK.
YOU ASKED FOR THIS.
AAAAAHH! I'M NOT EVEN A DOG!
AND I'M NOT BARKING!
PSHHHHH
PSHHHHH
I'M GOING TO HAVE TO STOP EVERY DOG IN THE NEIGHBOR-HOOD FROM BARKING.
THERE IS NO FURY LIKE THAT OF A SLEEP-DEPRIVED CAT. I'LL UNTIE YOU ALL ONCE JON GETS THIS COLLAR OFF ME.
NOW I'M GOING TO WATCH SOME TV AND WAIT FOR JON.
WFF
GFF
MFF
"OKAY, MAYBE MICE DON'T BARK PER SE.
"I WASN'T TAKING ANY CHANCES.

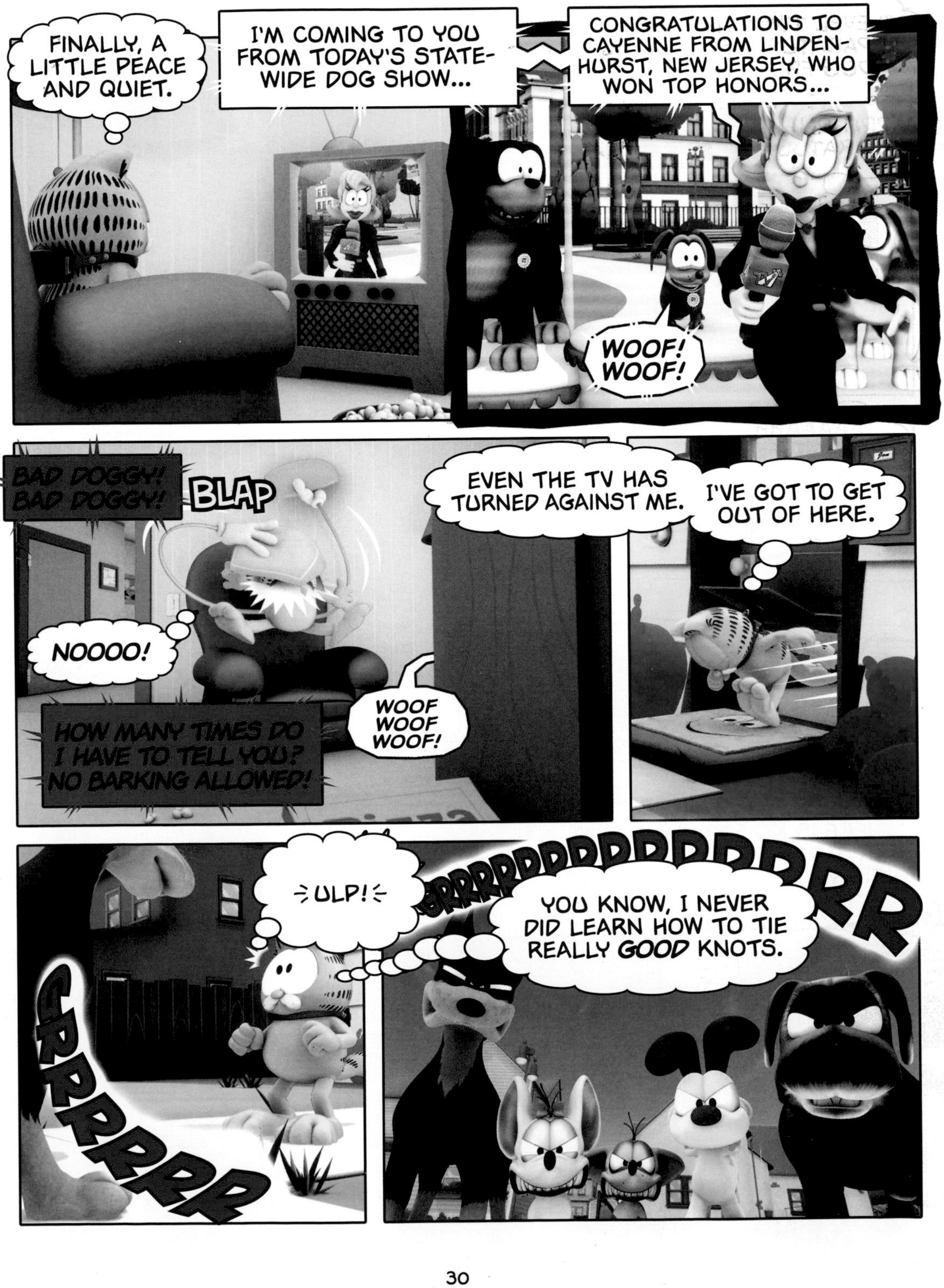
FINALLY, A LITTLE PEACE AND QUIET.
I'M COMING TO YOU FROM TODAY'S STATE-WIDE DOG SHOW...
CONGRATULATIONS TO CAYENNE FROM LINDEN-HURST, NEW JERSEY, WHO WON TOP HONORS...
WOOF! WOOF!
BAD DOGGY! BAD DOGGY!
BLAP
NOOOO!
HOW MANY TIMES DO I HAVE TO TELL YOU? NO BARKING ALLOWED!
WOOF WOOF WOOF!
EVEN THE TV HAS TURNED AGAINST ME.
I'VE GOT TO GET OUT OF HERE.
ULP!
GRRRRRRRRRRRRRRRR
YOU KNOW, I NEVER DID LEARN HOW TO TIE REALLY *GOOD* KNOTS.
GRRRRRRR

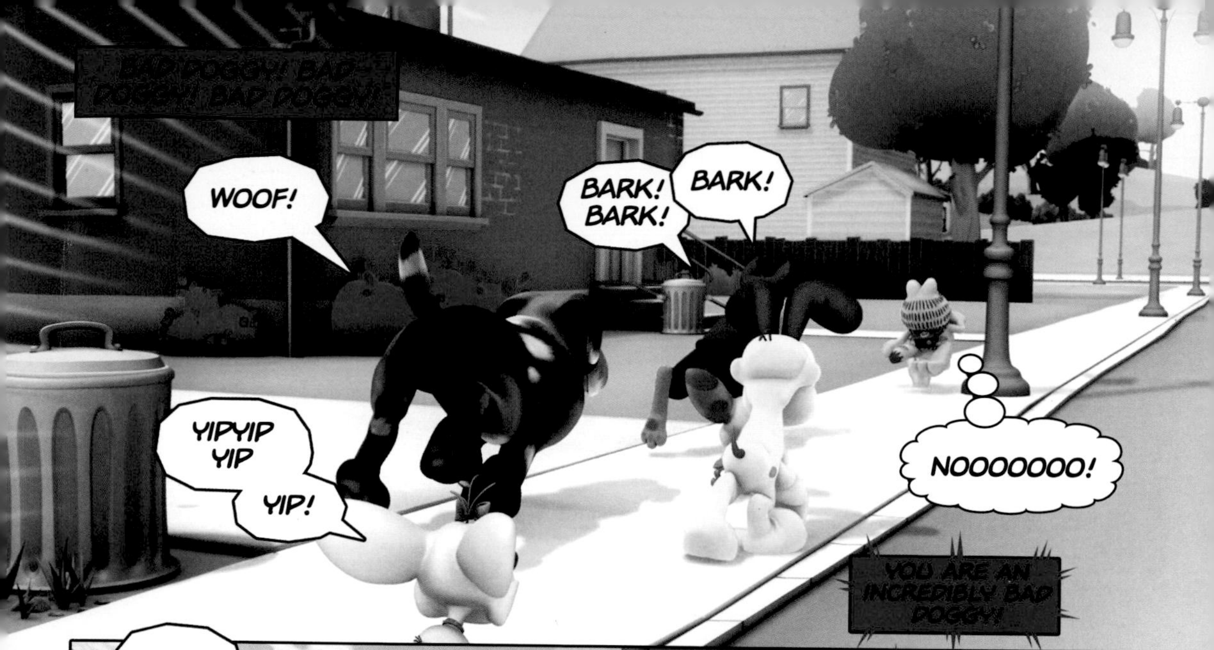
BAD DOGGY! BAD DOGGY! BAD DOGGY!
WOOF!
BARK! BARK!
BARK!
YIPYIP YIP
YIP!
NOOOOOOO!
YOU ARE AN INCREDIBLY BAD DOGGY!

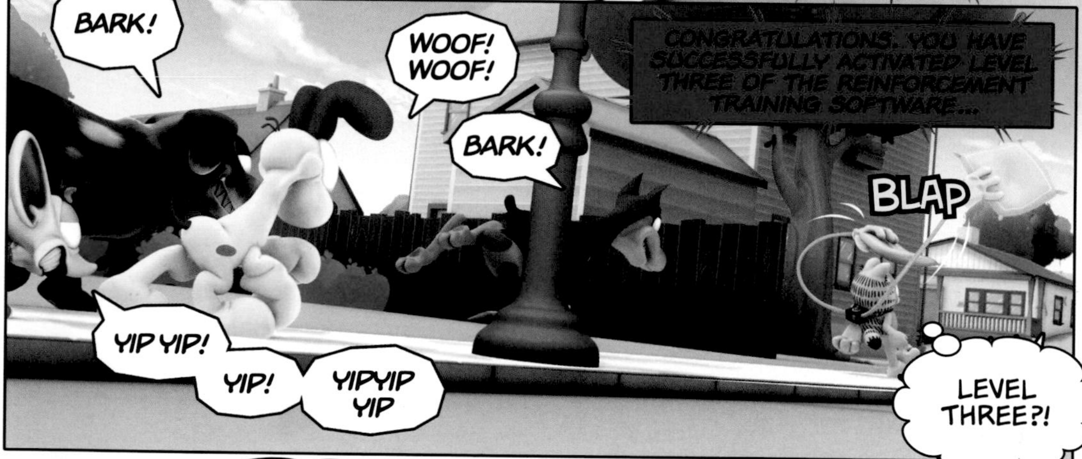
BARK!
WOOF! WOOF!
BARK!
CONGRATULATIONS. YOU HAVE SUCCESSFULLY ACTIVATED LEVEL THREE OF THE REINFORCEMENT TRAINING SOFTWARE...
BLAP
YIP YIP!
YIP!
YIPYIP YIP
LEVEL THREE?!

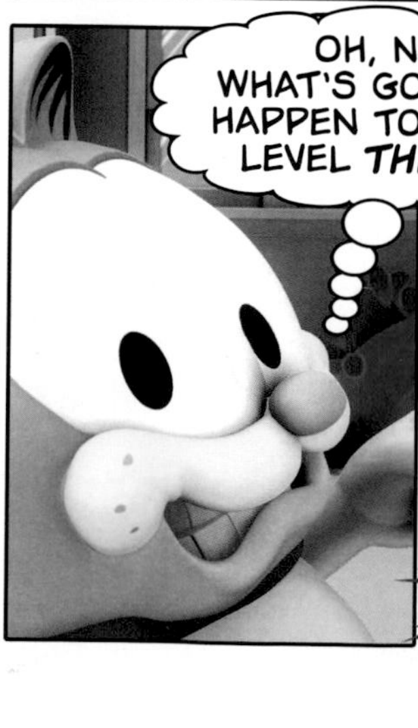
OH, NO! WHAT'S GOING TO HAPPEN TO ME ON LEVEL THREE?!

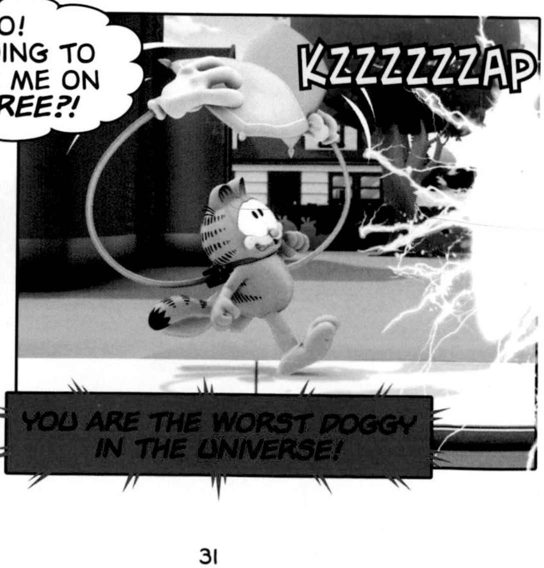
KZZZZZZAP
YOU ARE THE WORST DOGGY IN THE UNIVERSE!

"I DON'T REMEMBER WHAT HAPPENED NEXT...

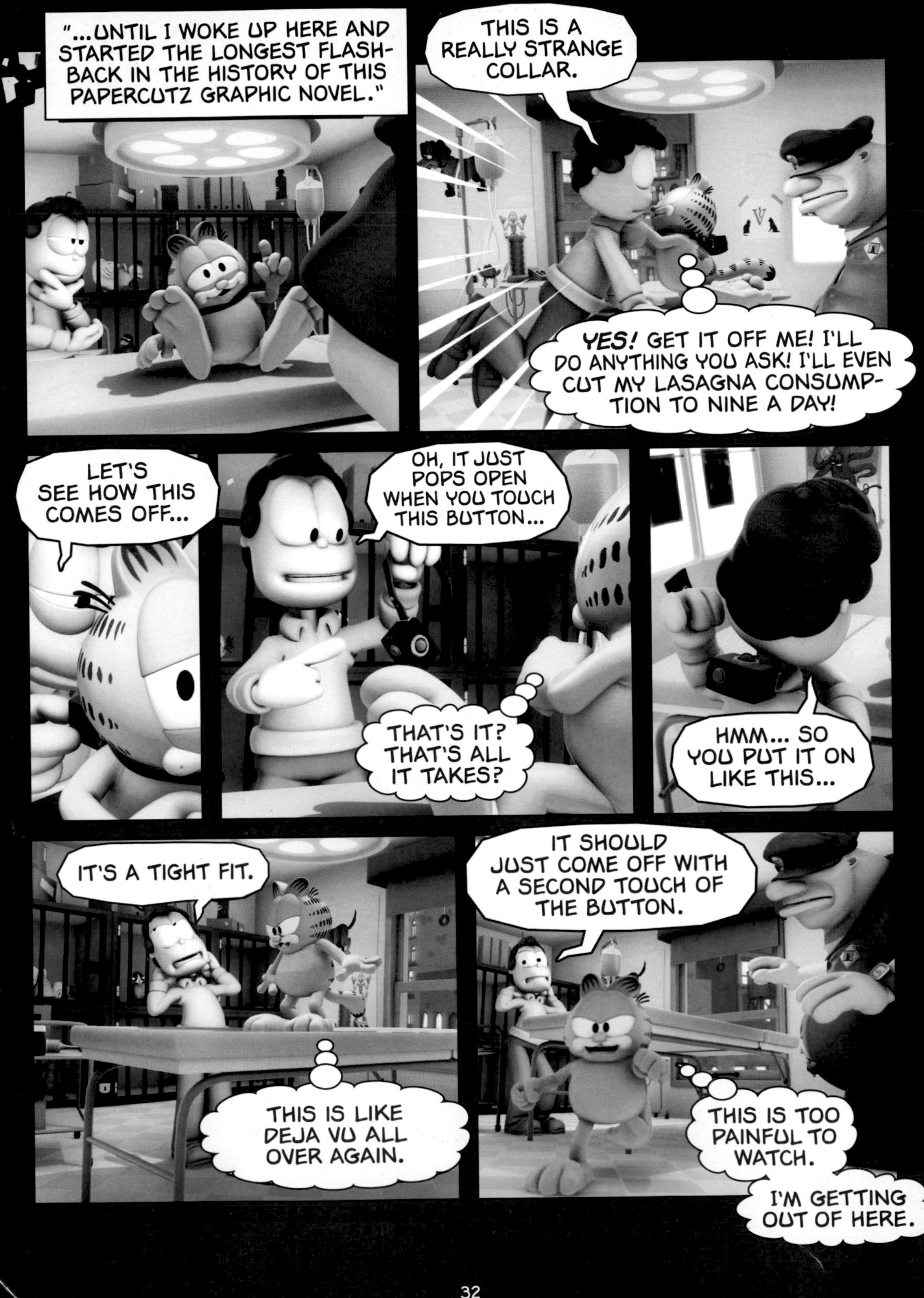

"...UNTIL I WOKE UP HERE AND STARTED THE LONGEST FLASH-BACK IN THE HISTORY OF THIS PAPERCUTZ GRAPHIC NOVEL."
THIS IS A REALLY STRANGE COLLAR.
YES! GET IT OFF ME! I'LL DO ANYTHING YOU ASK! I'LL EVEN CUT MY LASAGNA CONSUMP-TION TO NINE A DAY!
LET'S SEE HOW THIS COMES OFF...
OH, IT JUST POPS OPEN WHEN YOU TOUCH THIS BUTTON...
THAT'S IT? THAT'S ALL IT TAKES?
HMM... SO YOU PUT IT ON LIKE THIS...
IT'S A TIGHT FIT.
THIS IS LIKE DEJA VU ALL OVER AGAIN.
IT SHOULD JUST COME OFF WITH A SECOND TOUCH OF THE BUTTON.
THIS IS TOO PAINFUL TO WATCH.
I'M GETTING OUT OF HERE.

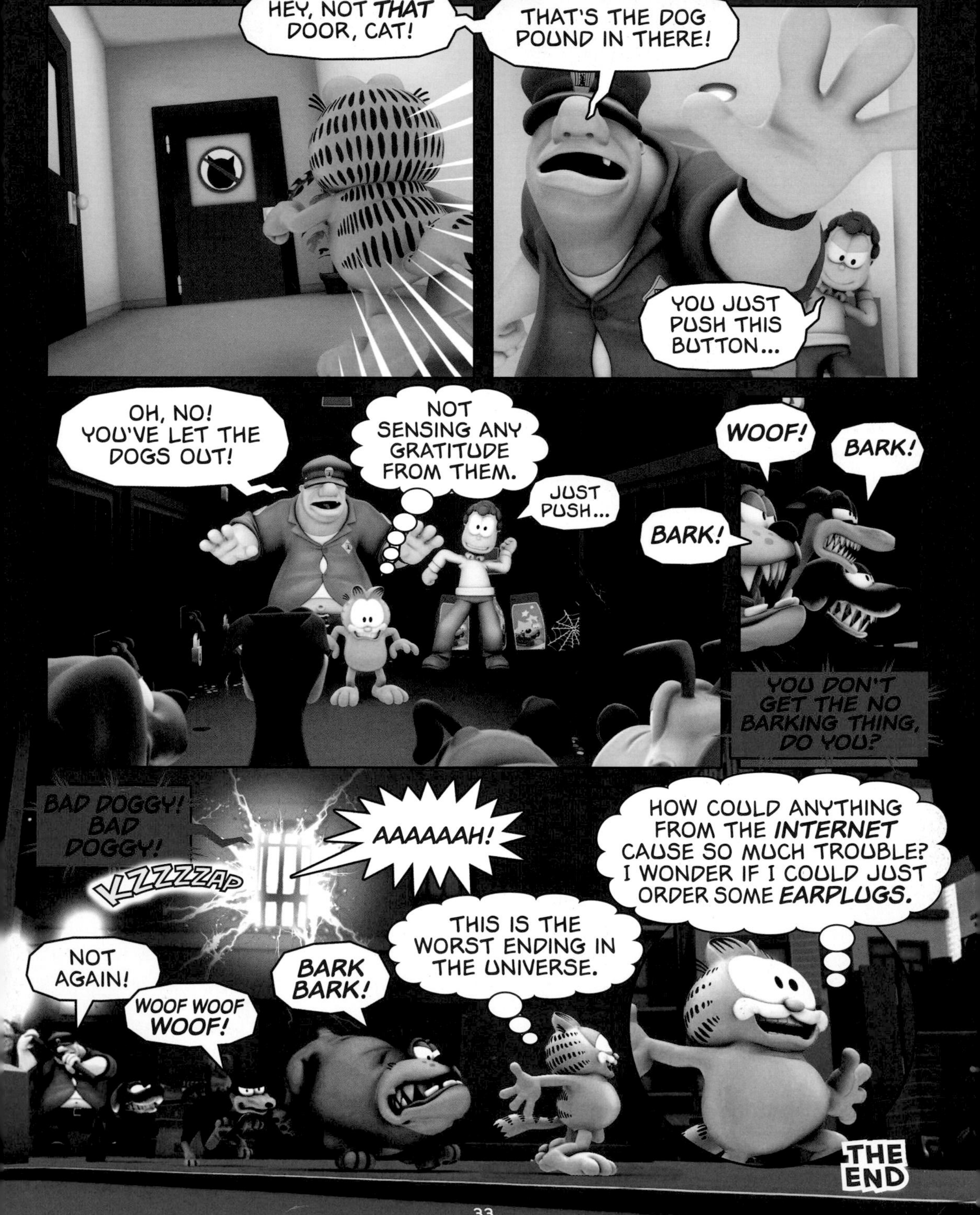
HEY, NOT THAT DOOR, CAT!
THAT'S THE DOG POUND IN THERE!
YOU JUST PUSH THIS BUTTON...
OH, NO! YOU'VE LET THE DOGS OUT!
NOT SENSING ANY GRATITUDE FROM THEM.
JUST PUSH...
WOOF!
BARK!
BARK!
YOU DON'T GET THE NO BARKING THING, DO YOU?
BAD DOGGY! BAD DOGGY!
KZZZZZAP
AAAAAAH!
HOW COULD ANYTHING FROM THE INTERNET CAUSE SO MUCH TROUBLE? I WONDER IF I COULD JUST ORDER SOME EARPLUGS.
THIS IS THE WORST ENDING IN THE UNIVERSE.
NOT AGAIN!
BARK BARK!
WOOF WOOF WOOF!
THE END

CARICATURE OF JIM
BY ORTHO

WATCH OUT FOR PAPERCUTZ™

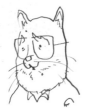

Welcome to the not-even-slightly stinky but altogether spooky sixth THE GARFIELD SHOW graphic novel from Papercutz, the only slightly scary boys and ghouls devoted to publishing great graphic novels for all ages. I'm Jim Salicrup, Editor-in-Chief and sometimes a somewhat stinky (from spending way too much time at his desk) skunk, here to talk about various things that come to mind after enjoying this particular volume of THE GARFIELD SHOW.

Speaking of which (not witch), for those of you who pay far too much attention and are wondering why this book's title is "Apprentice Sorcerer," instead of "Stink, Stank, Stunk," let's just say we changed our mind. If you look at page two of the first printing of THE GARFIELD SHOW #5 "Fido Food Feline," you'll see that we were indeed planning to call this volume "Stink, Stank, Stunk," but when we saw the artwork for the "Apprentice Sorcerer," we realized that would stand out from all our previous covers, in a really nice way. We hope you agree. (That, and at 30 pages, it takes up almost half of this graphic novel!)

Speaking of witches (not which), it seems Papercutz is now attracting almost as many witches as we are cats! One of our newest hits is an original graphic novel by Deb Lucke entitled "The Lunch Witch." Such an intriguing title may prompt you to ask, "What's it about?" We'll resist the very strong temptation to say "about 176 pages," and instead actually answer the question, by telling you exactly what it says on THE LUNCH WITCH page on Papercutz.com…

…For generations and generations, the women of Grunhilda's (She's the Lunch Witch!) family have stirred up trouble in a big, black pot. Grunhilda inherits her famous ancestors' recipes and cauldron, but no one believes in magic anymore. Despite the fact that Grunhilda's only useful skill is cooking up pots full of foul brew, she finds a job listing that might suit her: school lunch lady. She delights in scaring the kids until she meets Madison, a girl with thick glasses and unfinished homework who doesn't fit in. The two outsiders recognize each other. Madison needs help at school and at home, but helping people goes against everything Grunhilda's believes in as a witch! Will this girl be able to thaw the Lunch Witch's icy heart? Or will Grunhilda turn her back on a kindred spirit?

The Lunch Witch
Deb Lucke
PAPERCUTZ
1
The Lunch Witch
By Deb Lucke
PAPERCUTZ

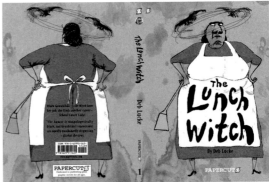

The Lunch Witch Copyright © 2016 by Deb Lucke

And that's the premise of the first volume of the all-new THE LUNCH WITCH graphic novel series from Papercutz. The critics have raved about THE LUNCH WITCH, and we're already publishing a second printing of the first volume to help meet demand. We suspect Abigail Cauldron would get along well with Grunhilda's frenemy Madison. And we strongly suspect that if you enjoyed "Apprentice Sorcerer," you'll enjoy THE LUNCH WITCH. You'll find THE LUNCH WITCH lurking at your favorite booksellers, probably somewhere near all THE GARFIELD SHOW graphic novels. Guess there's just something about cats and witches that just seems to go together!

Thanks, JIM

STAY IN TOUCH!

EMAIL:	SALICRUP@PAPERCUTZ.COM
WEB:	PAPERCUTZ.COM
TWITTER:	@PAPERCUTZGN
FACEBOOK:	PAPERCUTZGRAPHICNOVELS
BIRTHDAY CARDS:	PAPERCUTZ, 160 BROADWAY, SUITE 700, EAST WING, NEW YORK, NY 10038

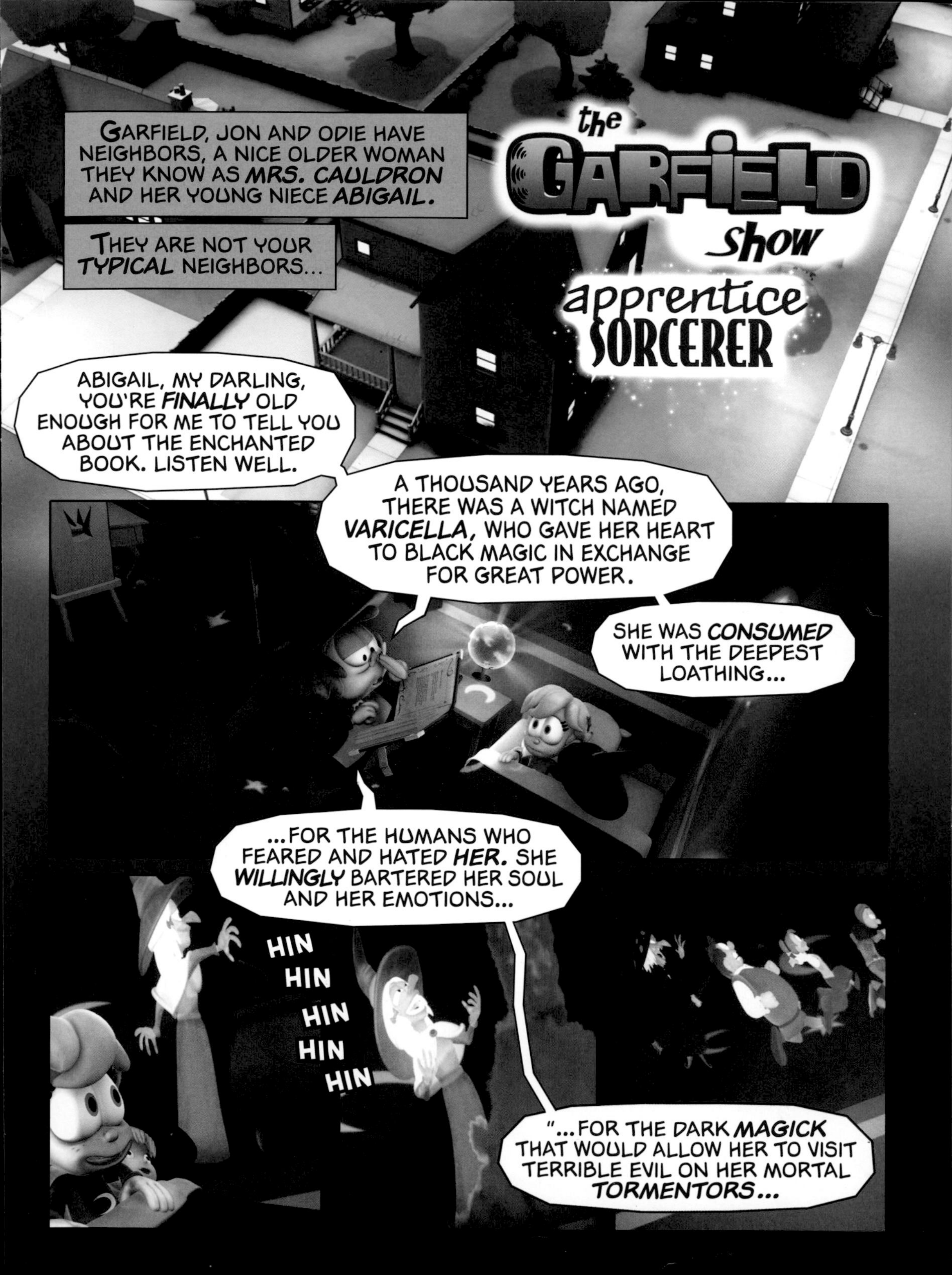
GARFIELD, JON AND ODIE HAVE NEIGHBORS, A NICE OLDER WOMAN THEY KNOW AS MRS. CAULDRON AND HER YOUNG NIECE ABIGAIL.
THEY ARE NOT YOUR TYPICAL NEIGHBORS...
the GARFIELD show
apprentice SORCERER
ABIGAIL, MY DARLING, YOU'RE FINALLY OLD ENOUGH FOR ME TO TELL YOU ABOUT THE ENCHANTED BOOK. LISTEN WELL.
A THOUSAND YEARS AGO, THERE WAS A WITCH NAMED VARICELLA, WHO GAVE HER HEART TO BLACK MAGIC IN EXCHANGE FOR GREAT POWER.
SHE WAS CONSUMED WITH THE DEEPEST LOATHING...
...FOR THE HUMANS WHO FEARED AND HATED HER. SHE WILLINGLY BARTERED HER SOUL AND HER EMOTIONS...
HIN HIN HIN HIN HIN
"...FOR THE DARK MAGICK THAT WOULD ALLOW HER TO VISIT TERRIBLE EVIL ON HER MORTAL TORMENTORS...

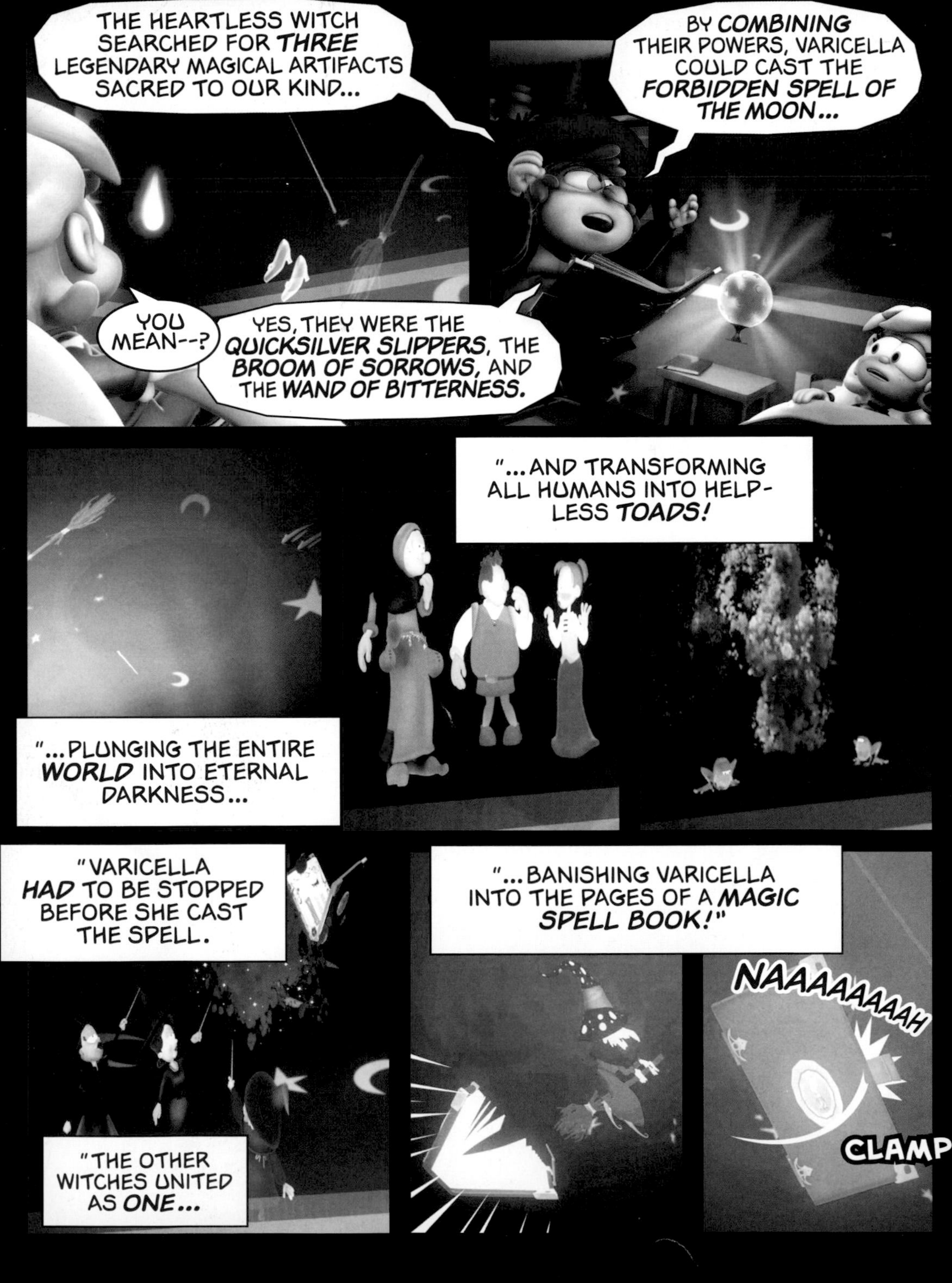
THE HEARTLESS WITCH SEARCHED FOR THREE LEGENDARY MAGICAL ARTIFACTS SACRED TO OUR KIND...
BY COMBINING THEIR POWERS, VARICELLA COULD CAST THE FORBIDDEN SPELL OF THE MOON...
YOU MEAN--?
YES, THEY WERE THE QUICKSILVER SLIPPERS, THE BROOM OF SORROWS, AND THE WAND OF BITTERNESS.
"...PLUNGING THE ENTIRE WORLD INTO ETERNAL DARKNESS...
"...AND TRANSFORMING ALL HUMANS INTO HELP-LESS TOADS!
"VARICELLA HAD TO BE STOPPED BEFORE SHE CAST THE SPELL.
"THE OTHER WITCHES UNITED AS ONE...
"...BANISHING VARICELLA INTO THE PAGES OF A MAGIC SPELL BOOK!"
NAAAAAAAAH
CLAMP

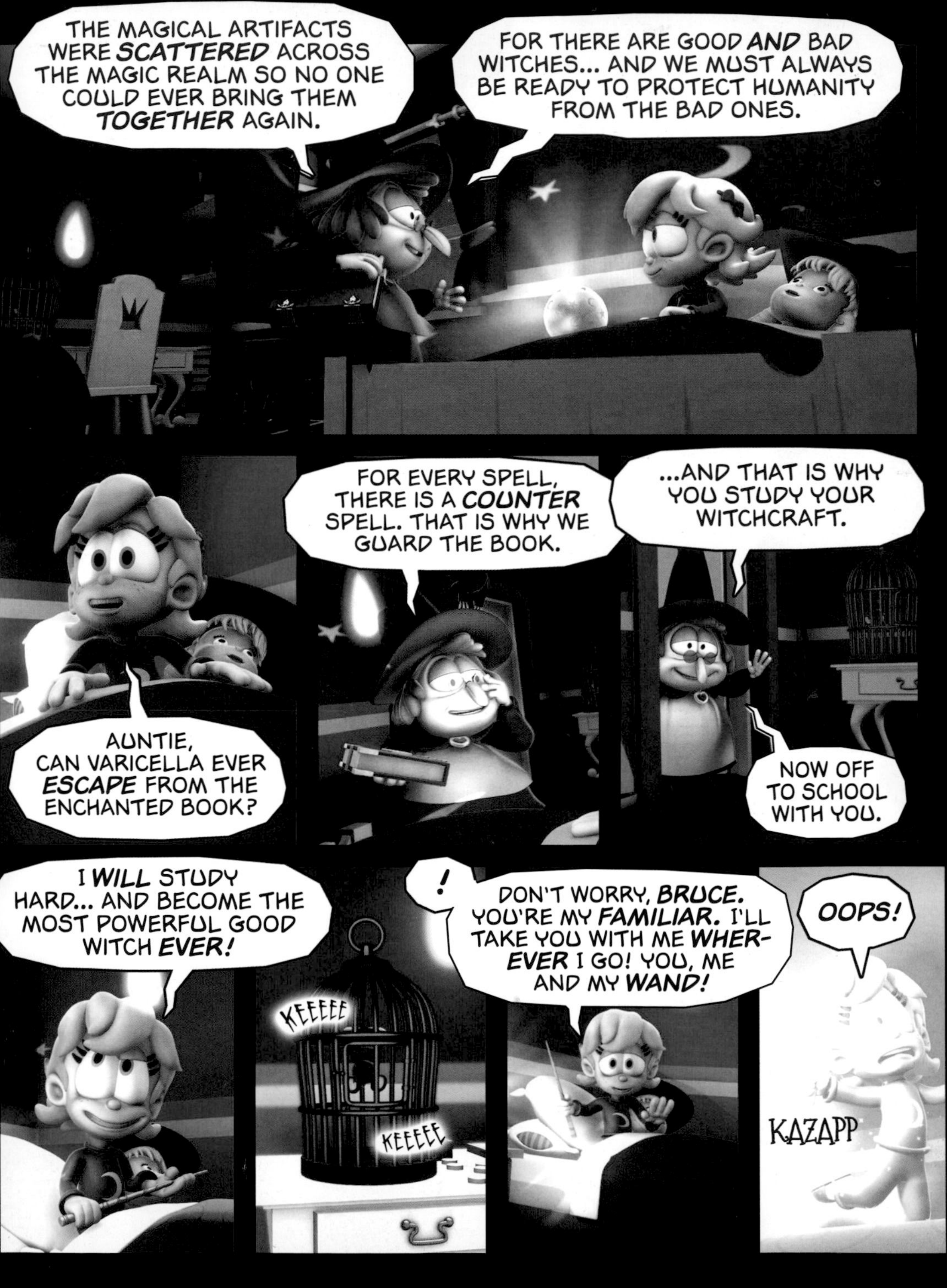
THE MAGICAL ARTIFACTS WERE SCATTERED ACROSS THE MAGIC REALM SO NO ONE COULD EVER BRING THEM TOGETHER AGAIN.
FOR THERE ARE GOOD AND BAD WITCHES... AND WE MUST ALWAYS BE READY TO PROTECT HUMANITY FROM THE BAD ONES.
AUNTIE, CAN VARICELLA EVER ESCAPE FROM THE ENCHANTED BOOK?
FOR EVERY SPELL, THERE IS A COUNTER SPELL. THAT IS WHY WE GUARD THE BOOK.
...AND THAT IS WHY YOU STUDY YOUR WITCHCRAFT.
NOW OFF TO SCHOOL WITH YOU.
I WILL STUDY HARD... AND BECOME THE MOST POWERFUL GOOD WITCH EVER!
KEEEEE
KEEEEE
!
DON'T WORRY, BRUCE. YOU'RE MY FAMILIAR. I'LL TAKE YOU WITH ME WHER-EVER I GO! YOU, ME AND MY WAND!
OOPS!
KAZAPP

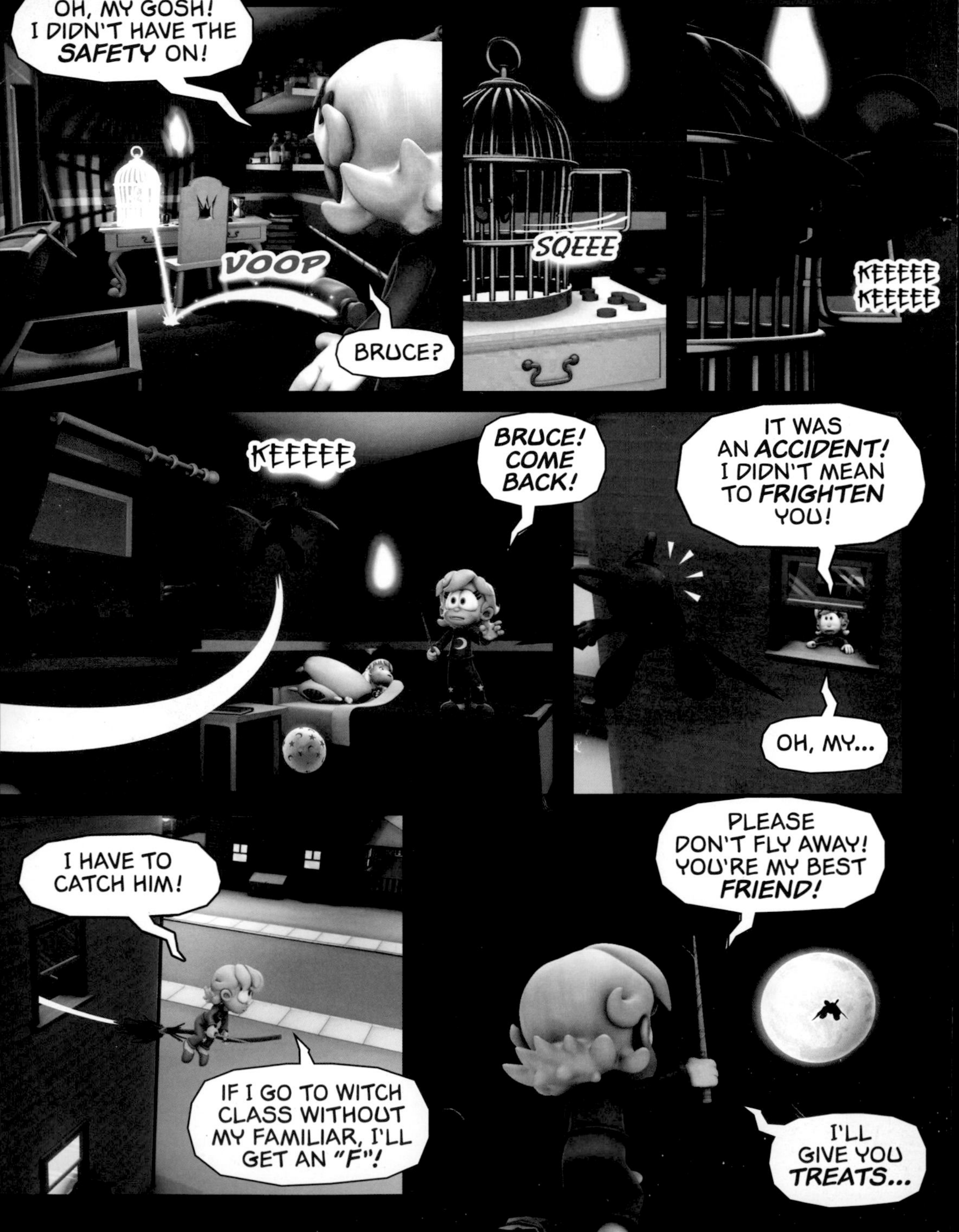
OH, MY GOSH! I DIDN'T HAVE THE SAFETY ON!
VOOP
BRUCE?
SQEEE
KEEEEE KEEEEE
KEEEEE
BRUCE! COME BACK!
IT WAS AN ACCIDENT! I DIDN'T MEAN TO FRIGHTEN YOU!
OH, MY...
I HAVE TO CATCH HIM!
IF I GO TO WITCH CLASS WITHOUT MY FAMILIAR, I'LL GET AN "F"!
PLEASE DON'T FLY AWAY! YOU'RE MY BEST FRIEND!
I'LL GIVE YOU TREATS...

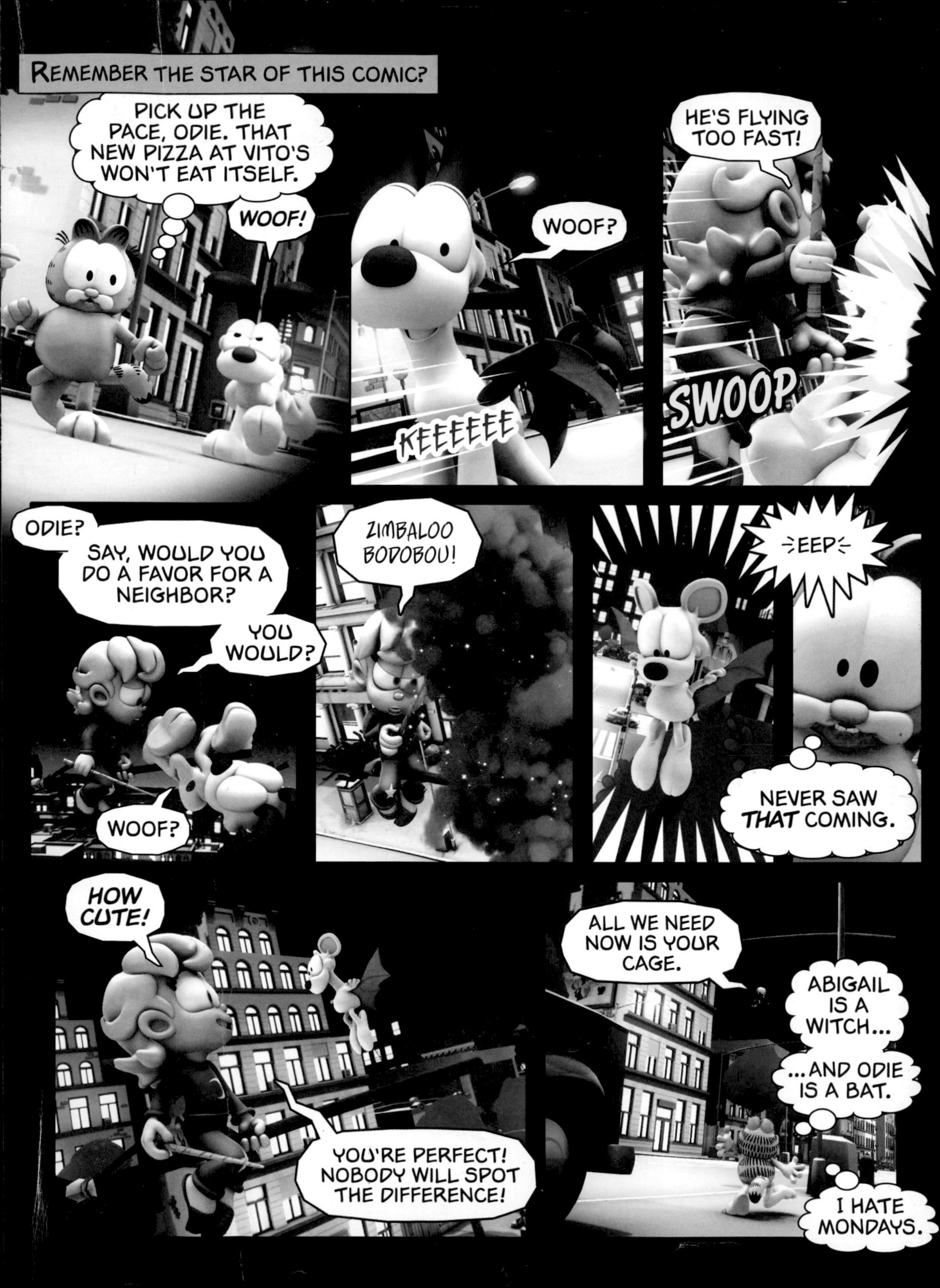
REMEMBER THE STAR OF THIS COMIC?
PICK UP THE PACE, ODIE. THAT NEW PIZZA AT VITO'S WON'T EAT ITSELF.
WOOF!
WOOF?
KEEEEEE
HE'S FLYING TOO FAST!
SWOOP
ODIE?
SAY, WOULD YOU DO A FAVOR FOR A NEIGHBOR?
YOU WOULD?
WOOF?
ZIMBALOO BODOBOU!
EEP
NEVER SAW *THAT* COMING.
HOW CUTE!
YOU'RE PERFECT! NOBODY WILL SPOT THE DIFFERENCE!
ALL WE NEED NOW IS YOUR CAGE.
ABIGAIL IS A WITCH...
...AND ODIE IS A BAT.
I HATE MONDAYS.

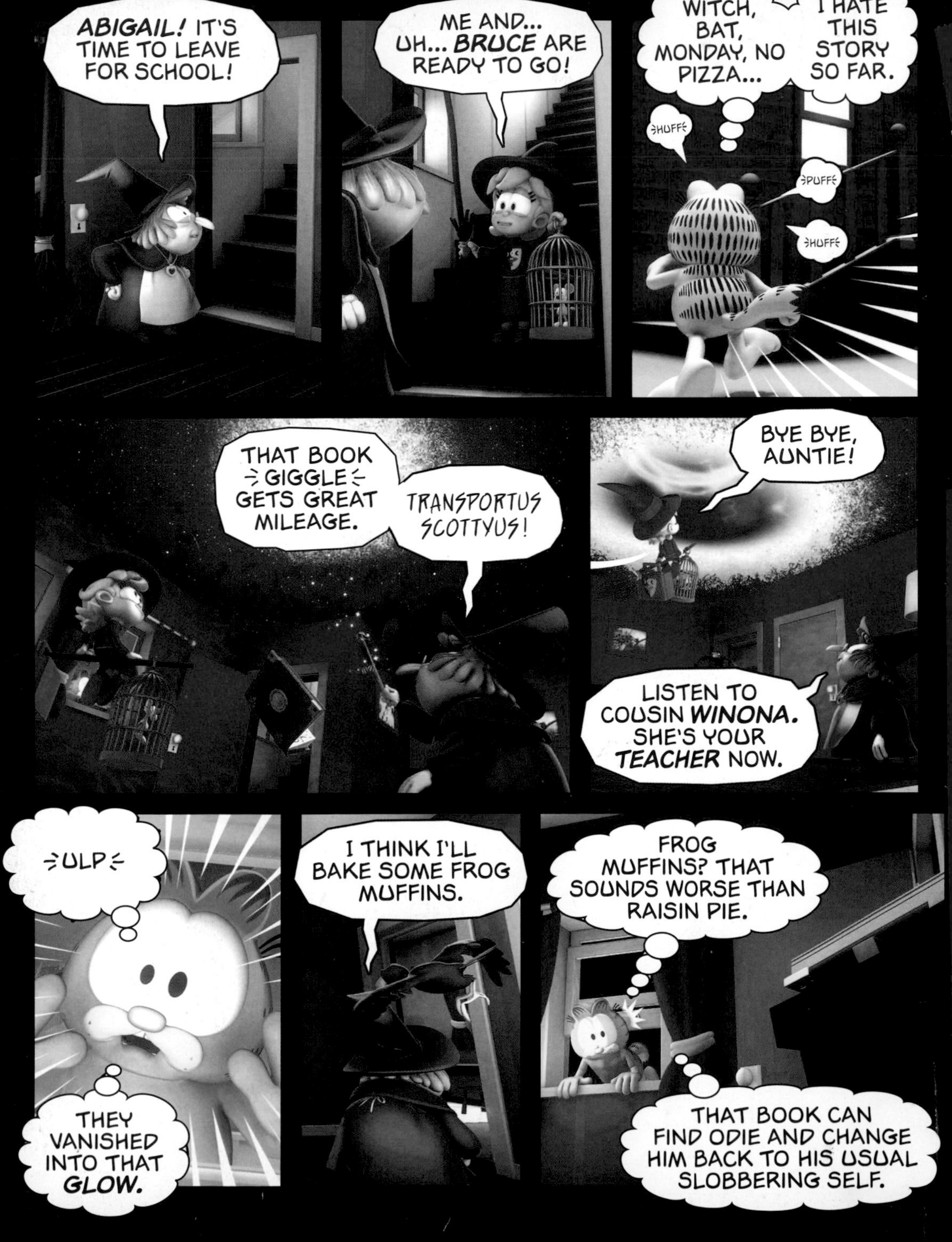
ABIGAIL! IT'S TIME TO LEAVE FOR SCHOOL!
ME AND... UH... BRUCE ARE READY TO GO!
WITCH, BAT, MONDAY, NO PIZZA...
I HATE THIS STORY SO FAR.
HUFF
PUFF
HUFF
THAT BOOK GIGGLE GETS GREAT MILEAGE.
TRANSPORTUS SCOTTYUS!
BYE BYE, AUNTIE!
LISTEN TO COUSIN WINONA. SHE'S YOUR TEACHER NOW.
ULP
THEY VANISHED INTO THAT GLOW.
I THINK I'LL BAKE SOME FROG MUFFINS.
FROG MUFFINS? THAT SOUNDS WORSE THAN RAISIN PIE.
THAT BOOK CAN FIND ODIE AND CHANGE HIM BACK TO HIS USUAL SLOBBERING SELF.

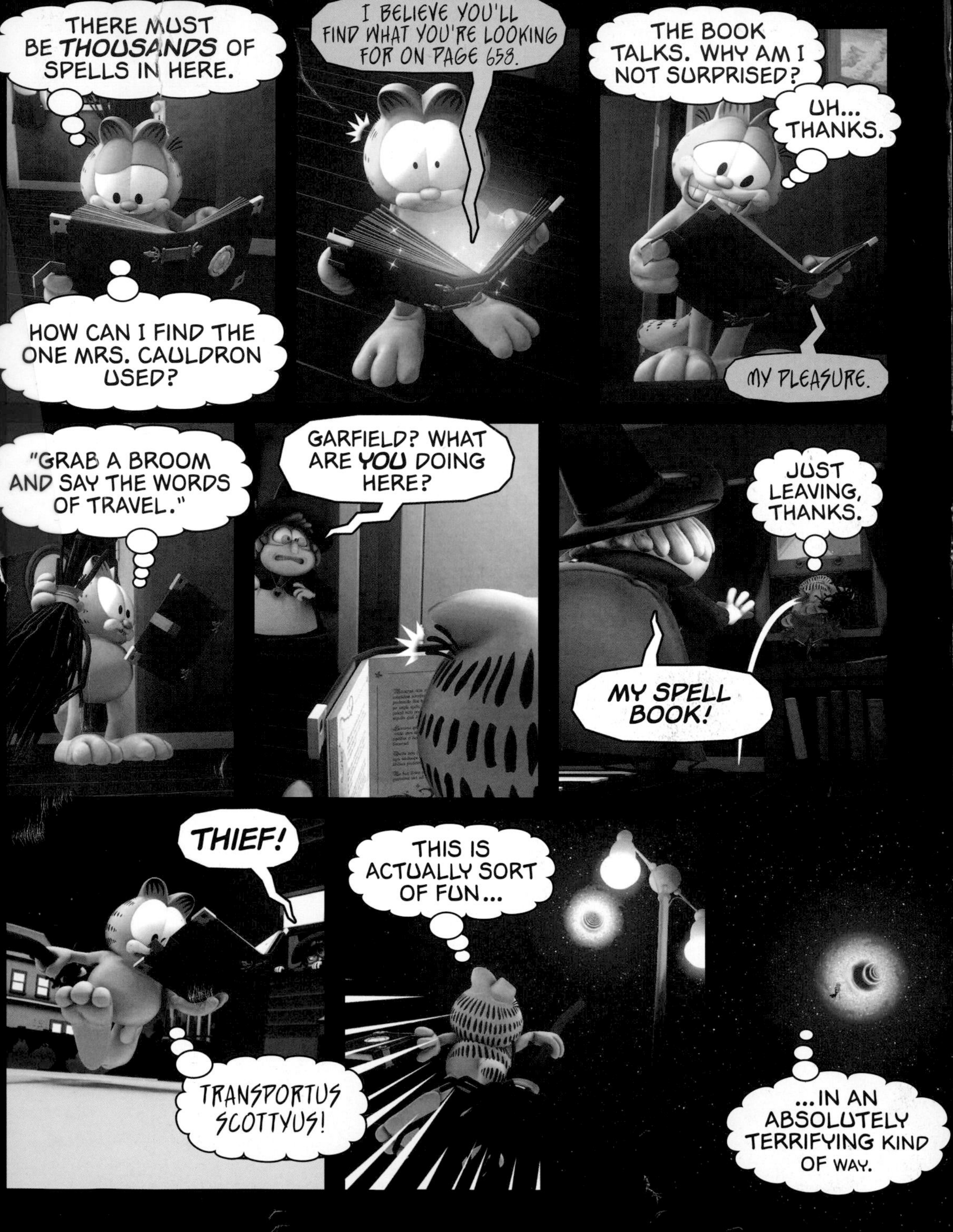
THERE MUST BE THOUSANDS OF SPELLS IN HERE.
HOW CAN I FIND THE ONE MRS. CAULDRON USED?
I BELIEVE YOU'LL FIND WHAT YOU'RE LOOKING FOR ON PAGE 658.
THE BOOK TALKS. WHY AM I NOT SURPRISED?
UH... THANKS.
MY PLEASURE.
"GRAB A BROOM AND SAY THE WORDS OF TRAVEL."
GARFIELD? WHAT ARE YOU DOING HERE?
JUST LEAVING, THANKS.
MY SPELL BOOK!
THIEF!
TRANSPORTUS SCOTTYUS!
THIS IS ACTUALLY SORT OF FUN...
...IN AN ABSOLUTELY TERRIFYING KIND OF WAY.

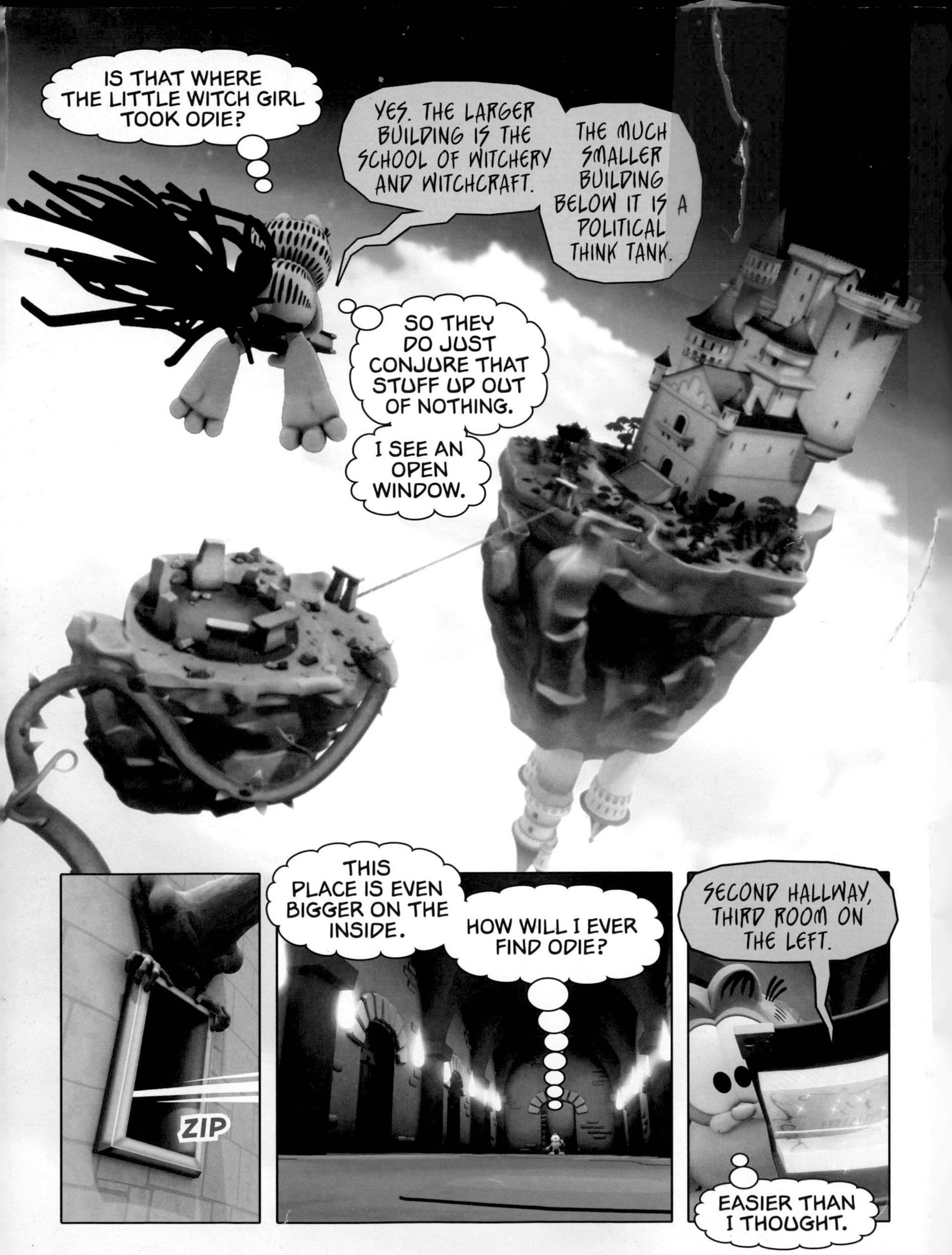
IS THAT WHERE THE LITTLE WITCH GIRL TOOK ODIE?
YES. THE LARGER BUILDING IS THE SCHOOL OF WITCHERY AND WITCHCRAFT.
THE MUCH SMALLER BUILDING BELOW IT IS A POLITICAL THINK TANK.
SO THEY DO JUST CONJURE THAT STUFF UP OUT OF NOTHING.
I SEE AN OPEN WINDOW.
ZIP
THIS PLACE IS EVEN BIGGER ON THE INSIDE.
HOW WILL I EVER FIND ODIE?
SECOND HALLWAY, THIRD ROOM ON THE LEFT.
EASIER THAN I THOUGHT.

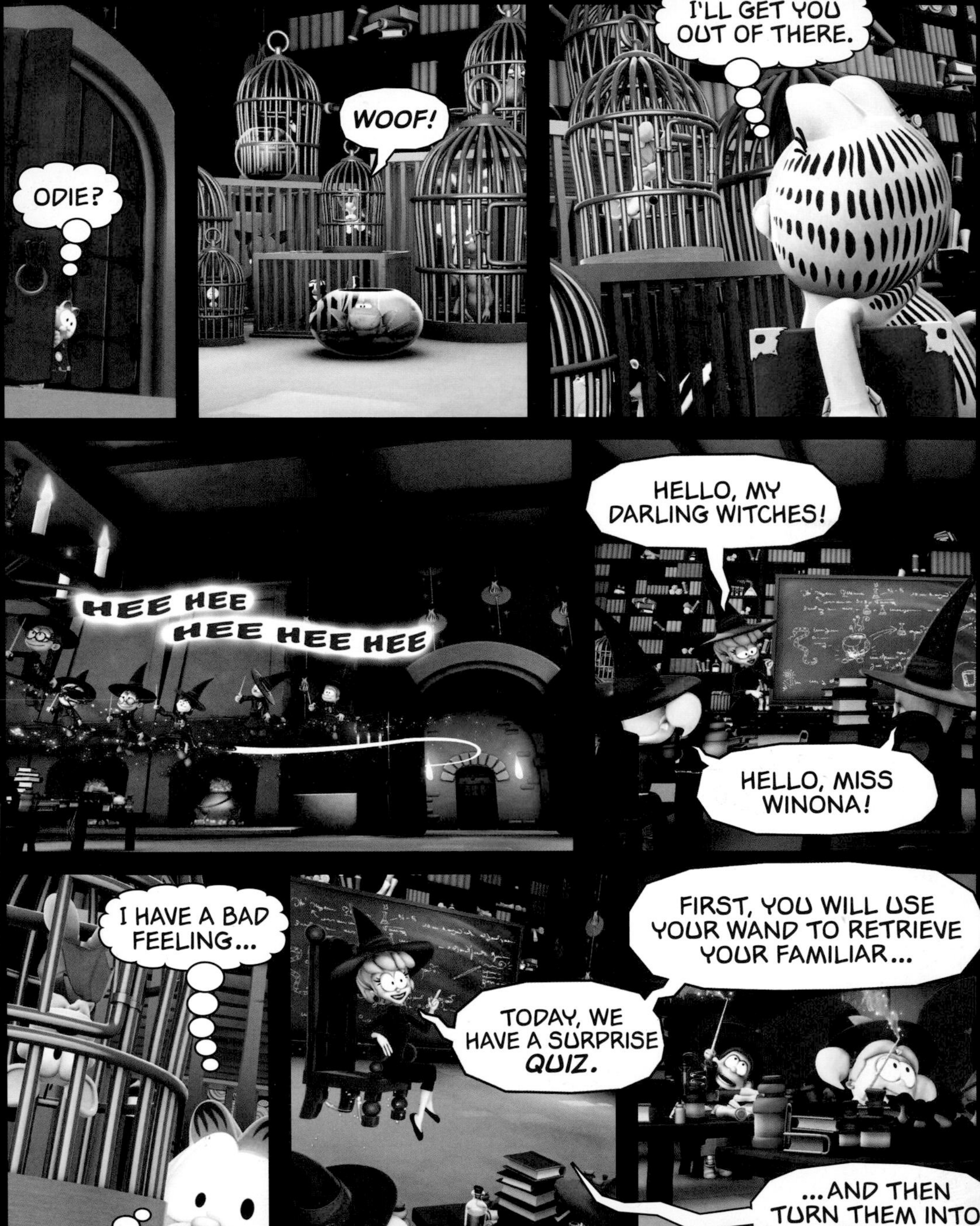
ODIE?
WOOF!
I'LL GET YOU OUT OF THERE.
HEE HEE
HEE HEE HEE HEE
HELLO, MY DARLING WITCHES!
HELLO, MISS WINONA!
I HAVE A BAD FEELING...
...ABOUT THIS.
TODAY, WE HAVE A SURPRISE *QUIZ.*
FIRST, YOU WILL USE YOUR WAND TO RETRIEVE YOUR FAMILIAR...
...AND THEN TURN THEM INTO A *TEACUP!*

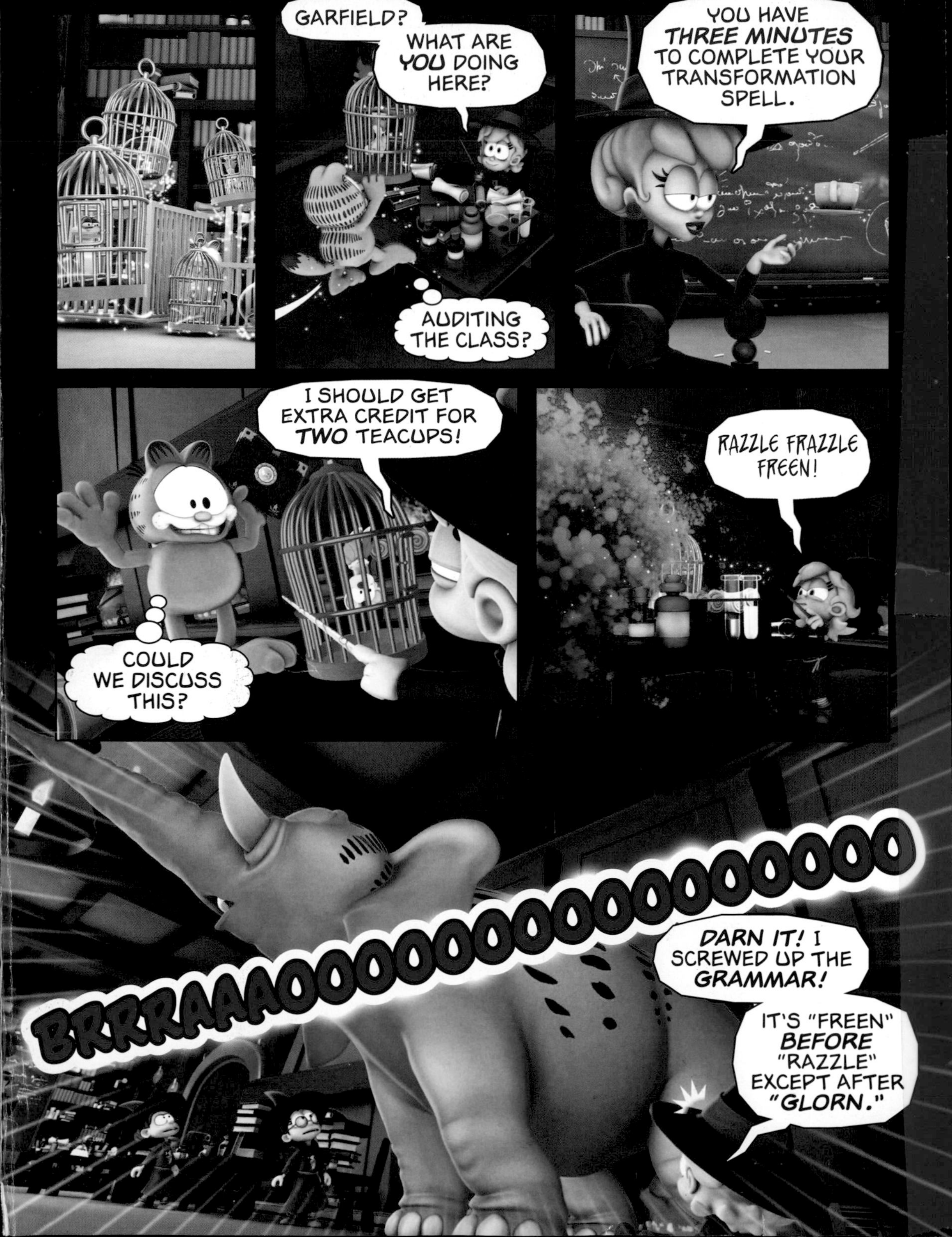
GARFIELD?
WHAT ARE YOU DOING HERE?
AUDITING THE CLASS?
YOU HAVE THREE MINUTES TO COMPLETE YOUR TRANSFORMATION SPELL.
I SHOULD GET EXTRA CREDIT FOR TWO TEACUPS!
COULD WE DISCUSS THIS?
RAZZLE FRAZZLE FREEN!
BRRRAAAOOOOOOOOOOOOOOOOOO
DARN IT! I SCREWED UP THE GRAMMAR!
IT'S "FREEN" BEFORE "RAZZLE" EXCEPT AFTER "GLORN."

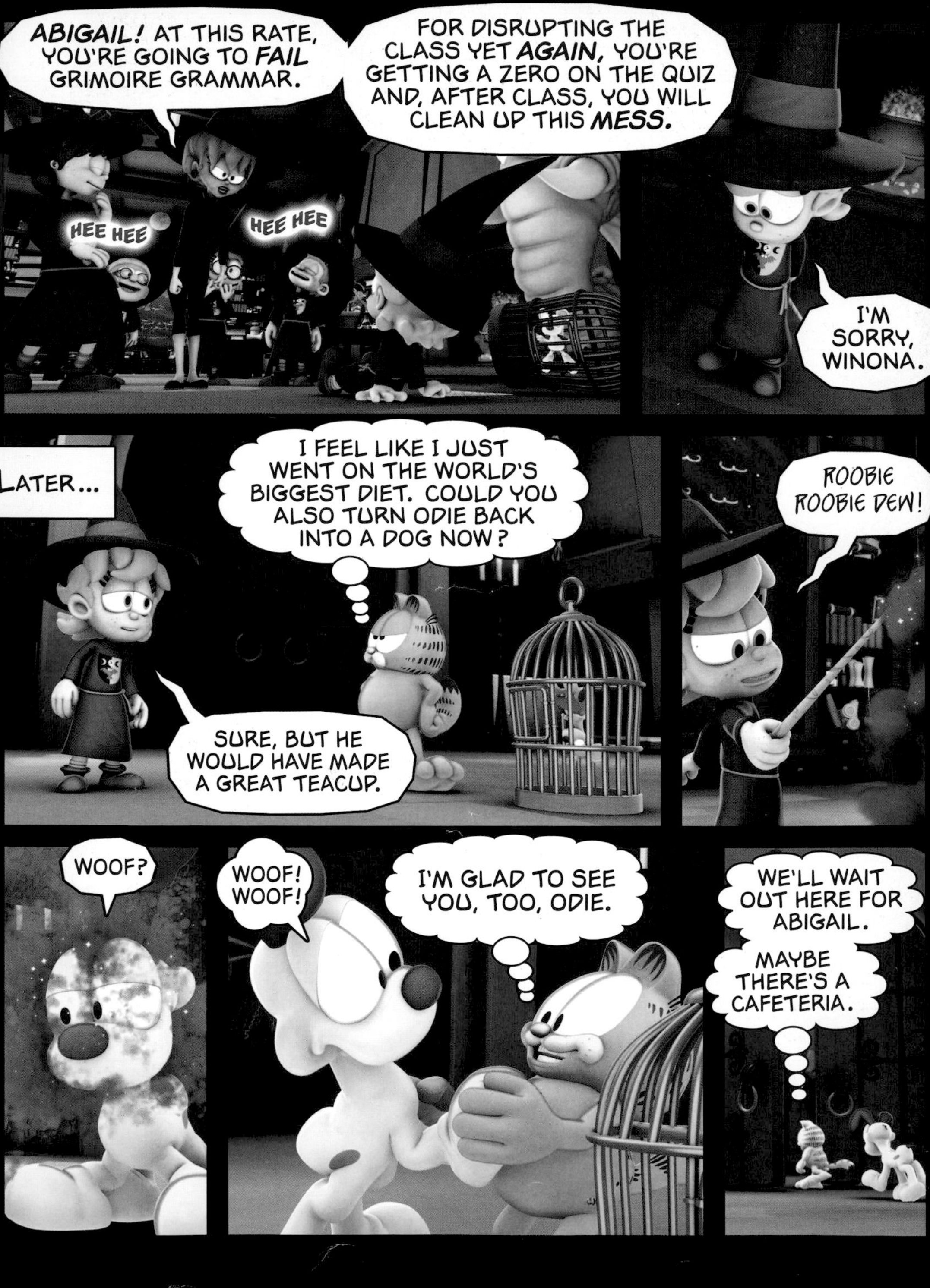

ABIGAIL! AT THIS RATE, YOU'RE GOING TO FAIL GRIMOIRE GRAMMAR.
FOR DISRUPTING THE CLASS YET AGAIN, YOU'RE GETTING A ZERO ON THE QUIZ AND, AFTER CLASS, YOU WILL CLEAN UP THIS MESS.
HEE HEE
HEE HEE
I'M SORRY, WINONA.
LATER...
I FEEL LIKE I JUST WENT ON THE WORLD'S BIGGEST DIET. COULD YOU ALSO TURN ODIE BACK INTO A DOG NOW?
SURE, BUT HE WOULD HAVE MADE A GREAT TEACUP.
ROOBIE ROOBIE DEW!
WOOF?
WOOF! WOOF!
I'M GLAD TO SEE YOU, TOO, ODIE.
WE'LL WAIT OUT HERE FOR ABIGAIL.
MAYBE THERE'S A CAFETERIA.

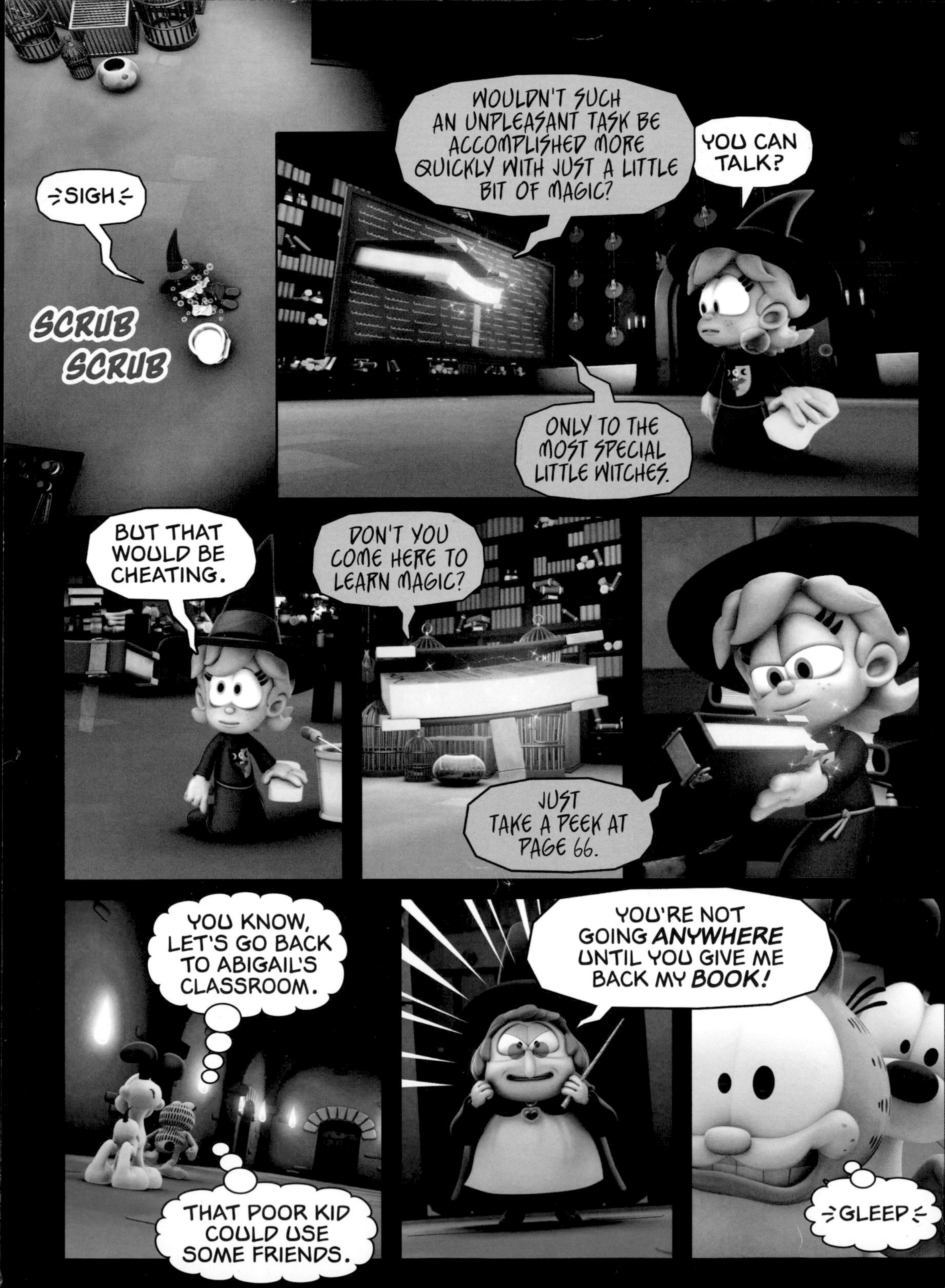
SIGH
SCRUB SCRUB
WOULDN'T SUCH AN UNPLEASANT TASK BE ACCOMPLISHED MORE QUICKLY WITH JUST A LITTLE BIT OF MAGIC?
YOU CAN TALK?
ONLY TO THE MOST SPECIAL LITTLE WITCHES.
BUT THAT WOULD BE CHEATING.
DON'T YOU COME HERE TO LEARN MAGIC?
JUST TAKE A PEEK AT PAGE 66.
YOU KNOW, LET'S GO BACK TO ABIGAIL'S CLASSROOM.
THAT POOR KID COULD USE SOME FRIENDS.
YOU'RE NOT GOING *ANYWHERE* UNTIL YOU GIVE ME BACK MY *BOOK!*
GLEEP

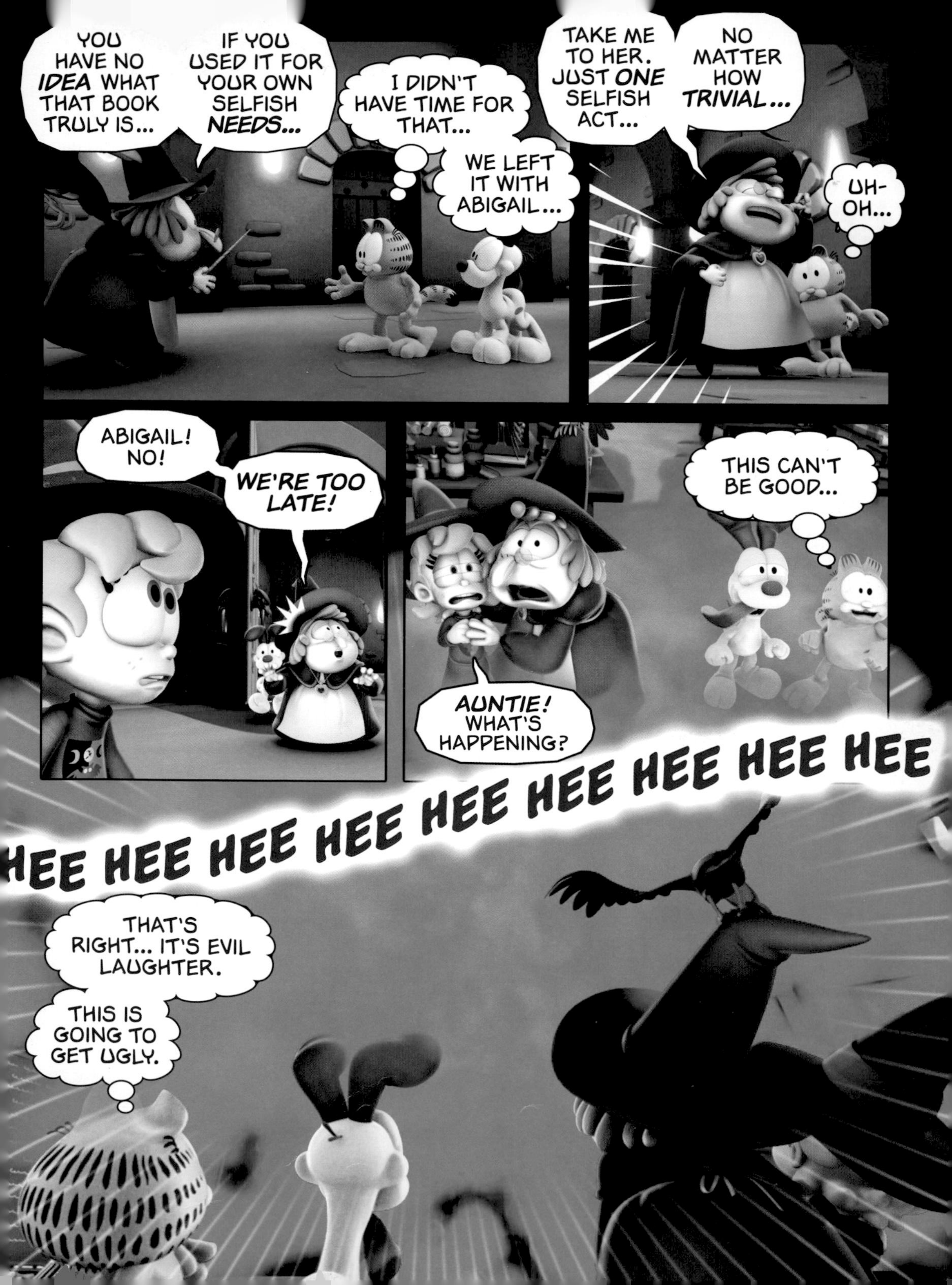
YOU HAVE NO IDEA WHAT THAT BOOK TRULY IS...
IF YOU USED IT FOR YOUR OWN SELFISH NEEDS...
I DIDN'T HAVE TIME FOR THAT...
WE LEFT IT WITH ABIGAIL...
TAKE ME TO HER. JUST ONE SELFISH ACT...
NO MATTER HOW TRIVIAL...
UH-OH...
ABIGAIL! NO!
WE'RE TOO LATE!
AUNTIE! WHAT'S HAPPENING?
THIS CAN'T BE GOOD...
HEE HEE HEE HEE HEE HEE HEE HEE HEE
THAT'S RIGHT... IT'S EVIL LAUGHTER.
THIS IS GOING TO GET UGLY.

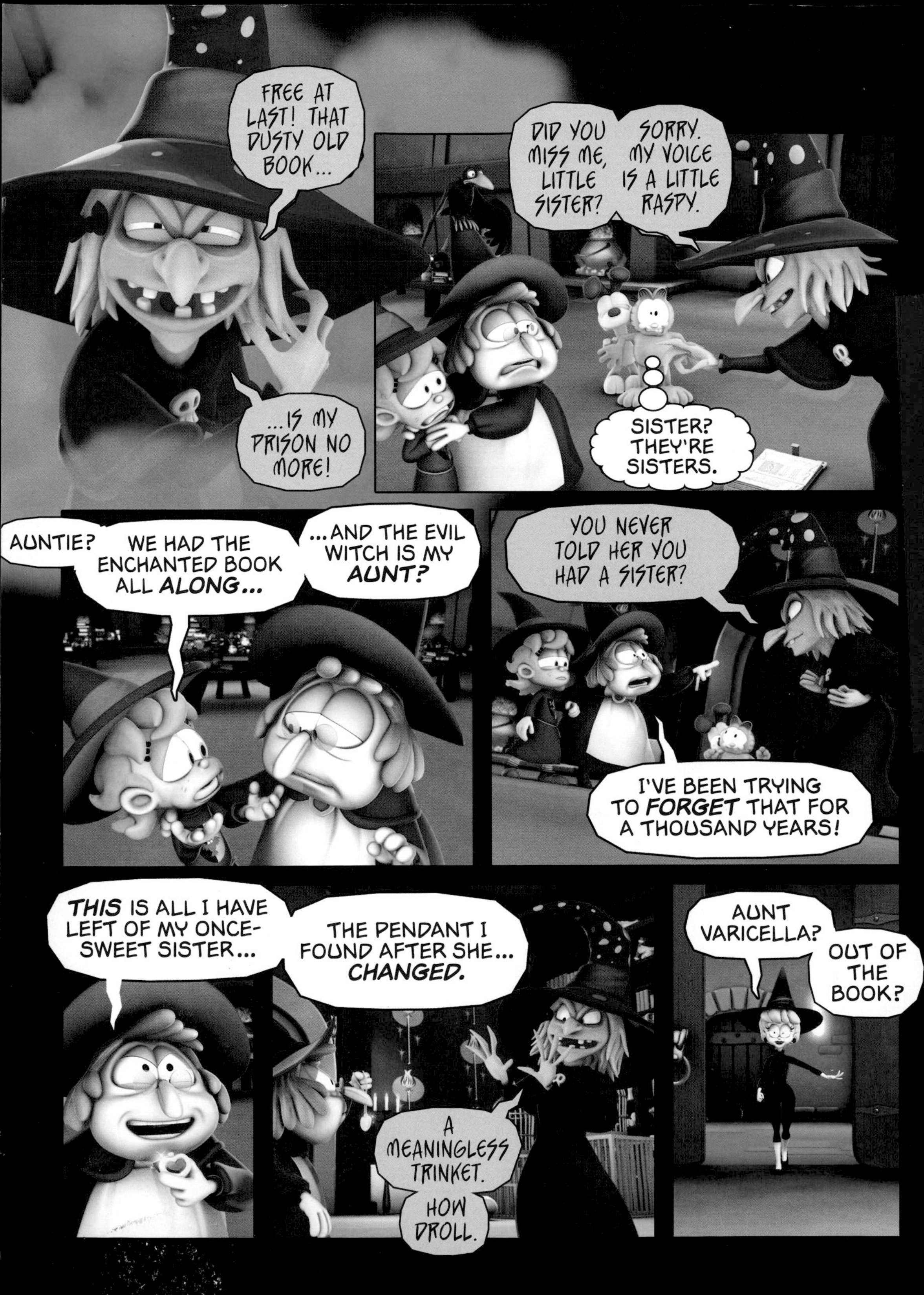
FREE AT LAST! THAT DUSTY OLD BOOK...
...IS MY PRISON NO MORE!
DID YOU MISS ME, LITTLE SISTER?
SORRY. MY VOICE IS A LITTLE RASPY.
SISTER? THEY'RE SISTERS.
AUNTIE?
WE HAD THE ENCHANTED BOOK ALL ALONG...
...AND THE EVIL WITCH IS MY AUNT?
YOU NEVER TOLD HER YOU HAD A SISTER?
I'VE BEEN TRYING TO FORGET THAT FOR A THOUSAND YEARS!
THIS IS ALL I HAVE LEFT OF MY ONCE-SWEET SISTER...
THE PENDANT I FOUND AFTER SHE... CHANGED.
A MEANINGLESS TRINKET.
HOW DROLL.
AUNT VARICELLA?
OUT OF THE BOOK?

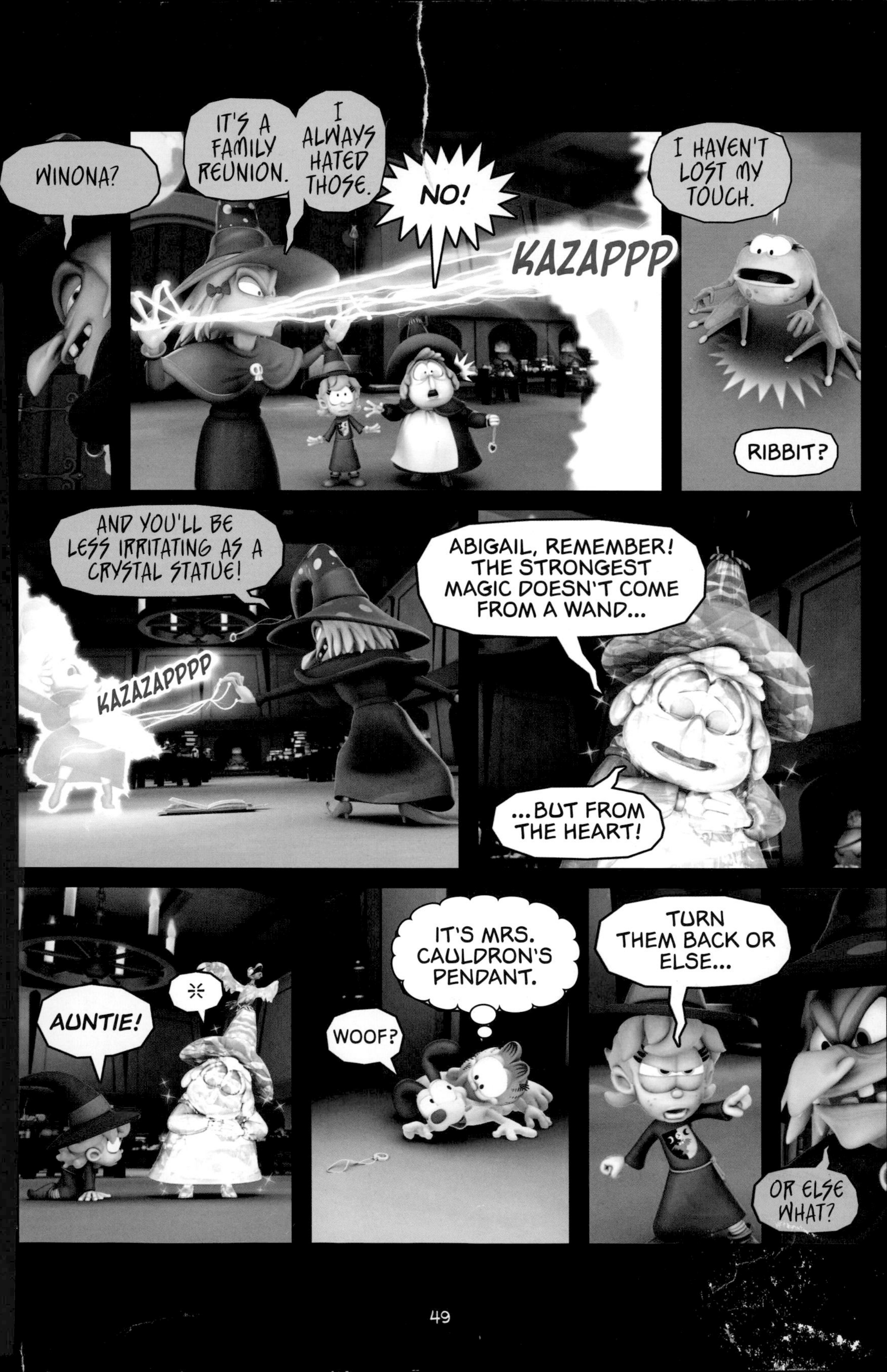
WINONA?
IT'S A FAMILY REUNION.
I ALWAYS HATED THOSE.
NO!
KAZAPPP
I HAVEN'T LOST MY TOUCH.
RIBBIT?
AND YOU'LL BE LESS IRRITATING AS A CRYSTAL STATUE!
KAZAZAPPPP
ABIGAIL, REMEMBER! THE STRONGEST MAGIC DOESN'T COME FROM A WAND...
...BUT FROM THE HEART!
AUNTIE!
WOOF?
IT'S MRS. CAULDRON'S PENDANT.
TURN THEM BACK OR ELSE...
OR ELSE WHAT?

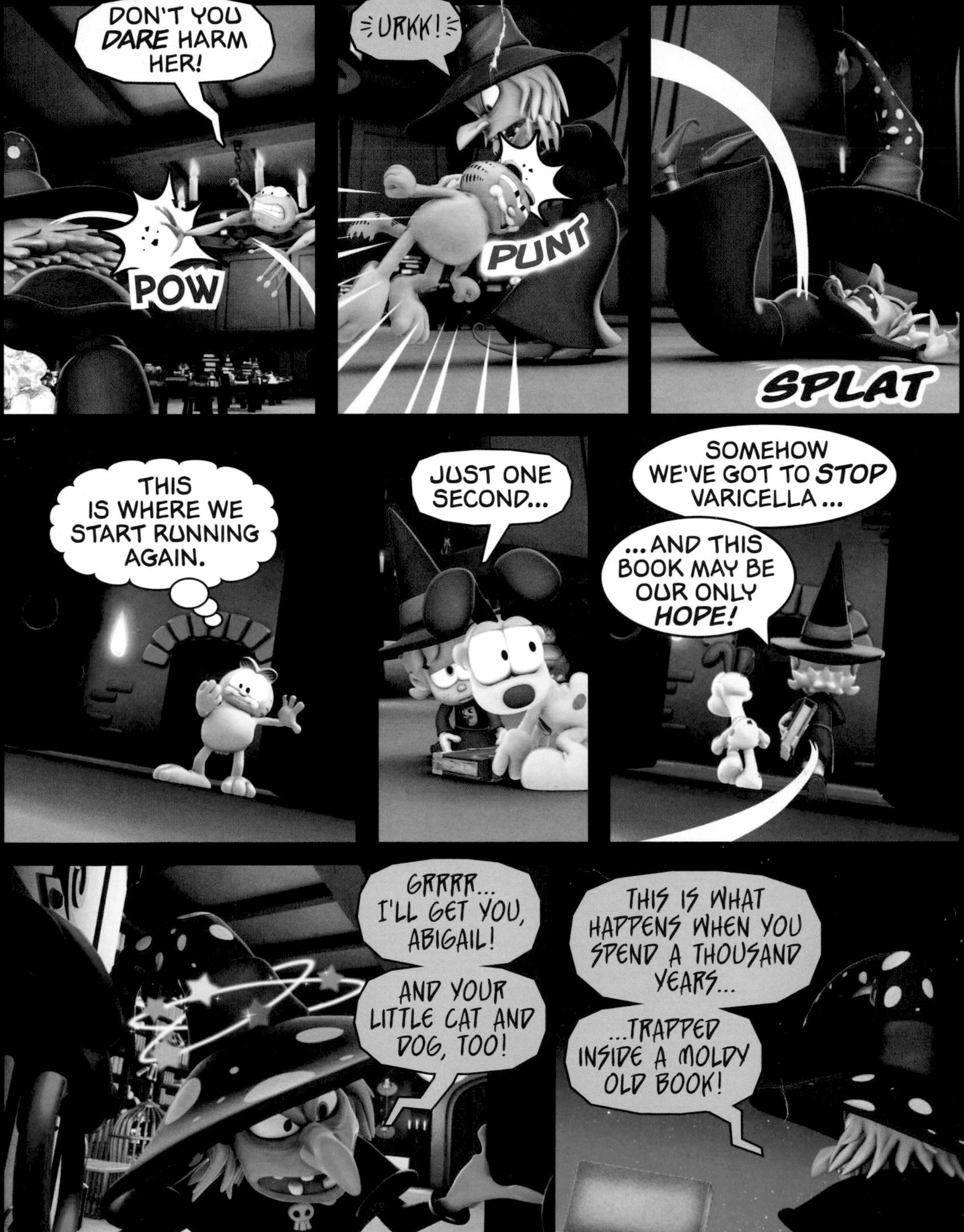
DON'T YOU DARE HARM HER!
POW
URKK!
PUNT
SPLAT
THIS IS WHERE WE START RUNNING AGAIN.
JUST ONE SECOND...
SOMEHOW WE'VE GOT TO STOP VARICELLA...
...AND THIS BOOK MAY BE OUR ONLY HOPE!
GRRRR... I'LL GET YOU, ABIGAIL!
AND YOUR LITTLE CAT AND DOG, TOO!
THIS IS WHAT HAPPENS WHEN YOU SPEND A THOUSAND YEARS...
...TRAPPED INSIDE A MOLDY OLD BOOK!

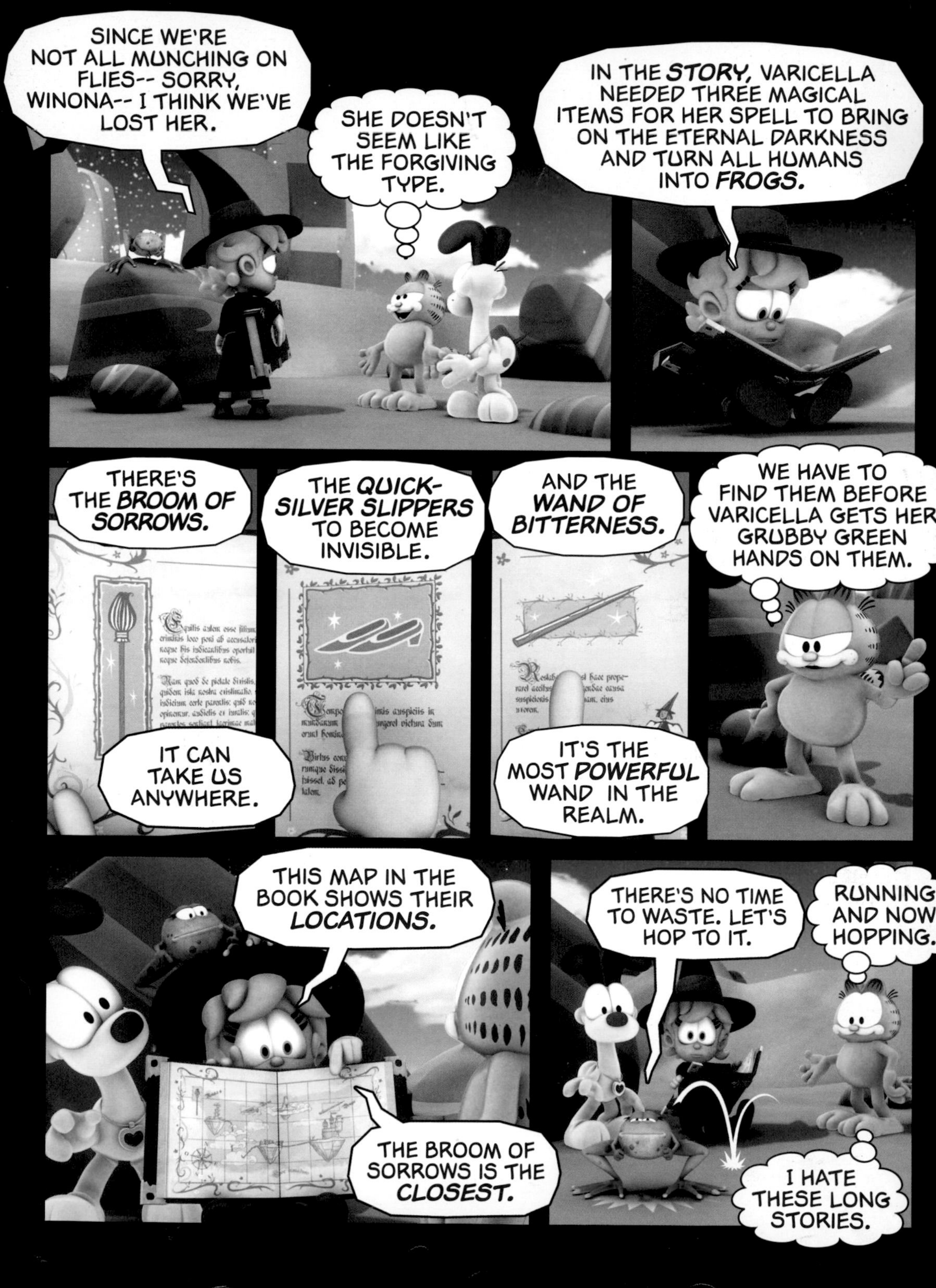

SINCE WE'RE NOT ALL MUNCHING ON FLIES-- SORRY, WINONA-- I THINK WE'VE LOST HER.
SHE DOESN'T SEEM LIKE THE FORGIVING TYPE.
IN THE STORY, VARICELLA NEEDED THREE MAGICAL ITEMS FOR HER SPELL TO BRING ON THE ETERNAL DARKNESS AND TURN ALL HUMANS INTO FROGS.
THERE'S THE BROOM OF SORROWS.
IT CAN TAKE US ANYWHERE.
THE QUICK-SILVER SLIPPERS TO BECOME INVISIBLE.
AND THE WAND OF BITTERNESS.
IT'S THE MOST POWERFUL WAND IN THE REALM.
WE HAVE TO FIND THEM BEFORE VARICELLA GETS HER GRUBBY GREEN HANDS ON THEM.
THIS MAP IN THE BOOK SHOWS THEIR LOCATIONS.
THE BROOM OF SORROWS IS THE CLOSEST.
THERE'S NO TIME TO WASTE. LET'S HOP TO IT.
RUNNING AND NOW HOPPING.
I HATE THESE LONG STORIES.

ONE SHORT HOUR LATER...
THE BROOM OF SORROWS IS HERE, HIDDEN DEEP WITHIN THE SNARLING FOREST...
I JUST REMEMBERED SOMETHING...
THIS IS WHERE WE CUT DOWN TREES TO MAKE BROOMS AND WANDS. WITCHES AREN'T WELCOME HERE.
THE REMAINING TREES CONSIDER US THEIR ENEMIES.
TREES? WHAT CAN TREES DO TO US?
WHY DO I ASK SUCH QUESTIONS?
BRROOAAAAARRRRRRRRRRRRRR
THE TRESS ARE MOVING.
OF COURSE THEY ARE.
SIGH.

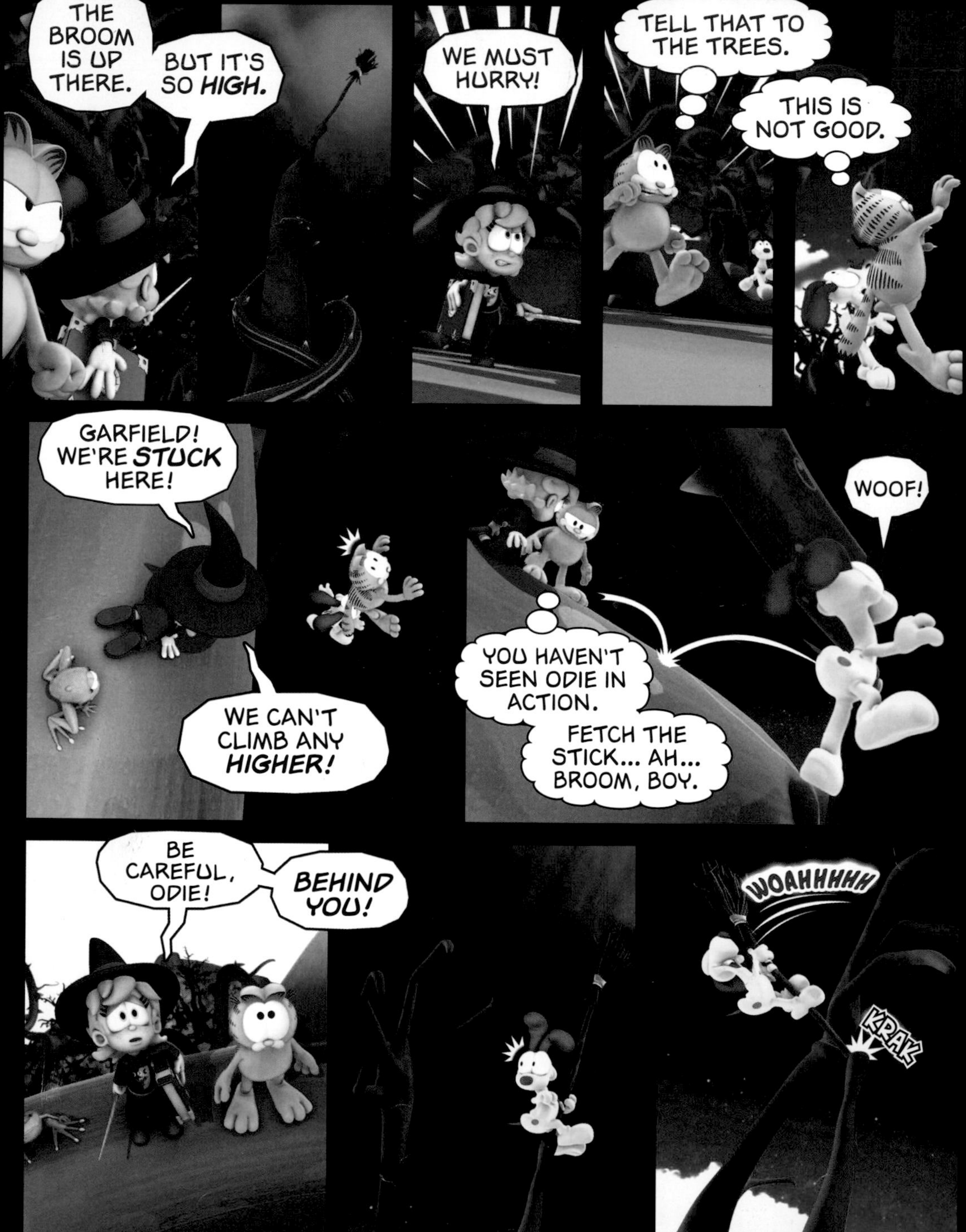
THE BROOM IS UP THERE.
BUT IT'S SO HIGH.
WE MUST HURRY!
TELL THAT TO THE TREES.
THIS IS NOT GOOD.
GARFIELD! WE'RE STUCK HERE!
WE CAN'T CLIMB ANY HIGHER!
WOOF!
YOU HAVEN'T SEEN ODIE IN ACTION.
FETCH THE STICK... AH... BROOM, BOY.
BE CAREFUL, ODIE!
BEHIND YOU!
WOAHHHHH
KRAK

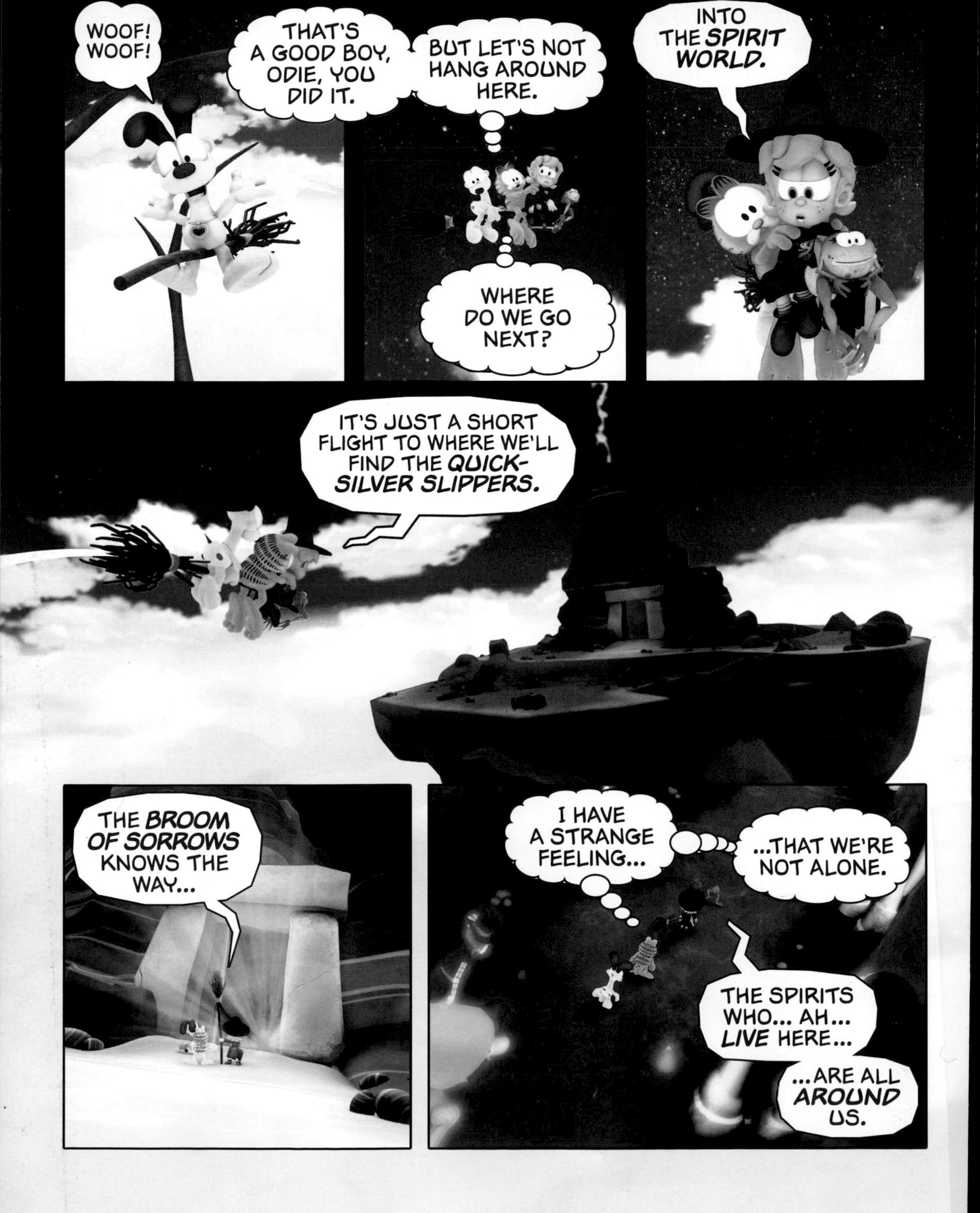
WOOF! WOOF!
THAT'S A GOOD BOY, ODIE, YOU DID IT.
BUT LET'S NOT HANG AROUND HERE.
WHERE DO WE GO NEXT?
INTO THE SPIRIT WORLD.
IT'S JUST A SHORT FLIGHT TO WHERE WE'LL FIND THE QUICK-SILVER SLIPPERS.
THE BROOM OF SORROWS KNOWS THE WAY...
I HAVE A STRANGE FEELING...
...THAT WE'RE NOT ALONE.
THE SPIRITS WHO... AH... LIVE HERE...
...ARE ALL AROUND US.

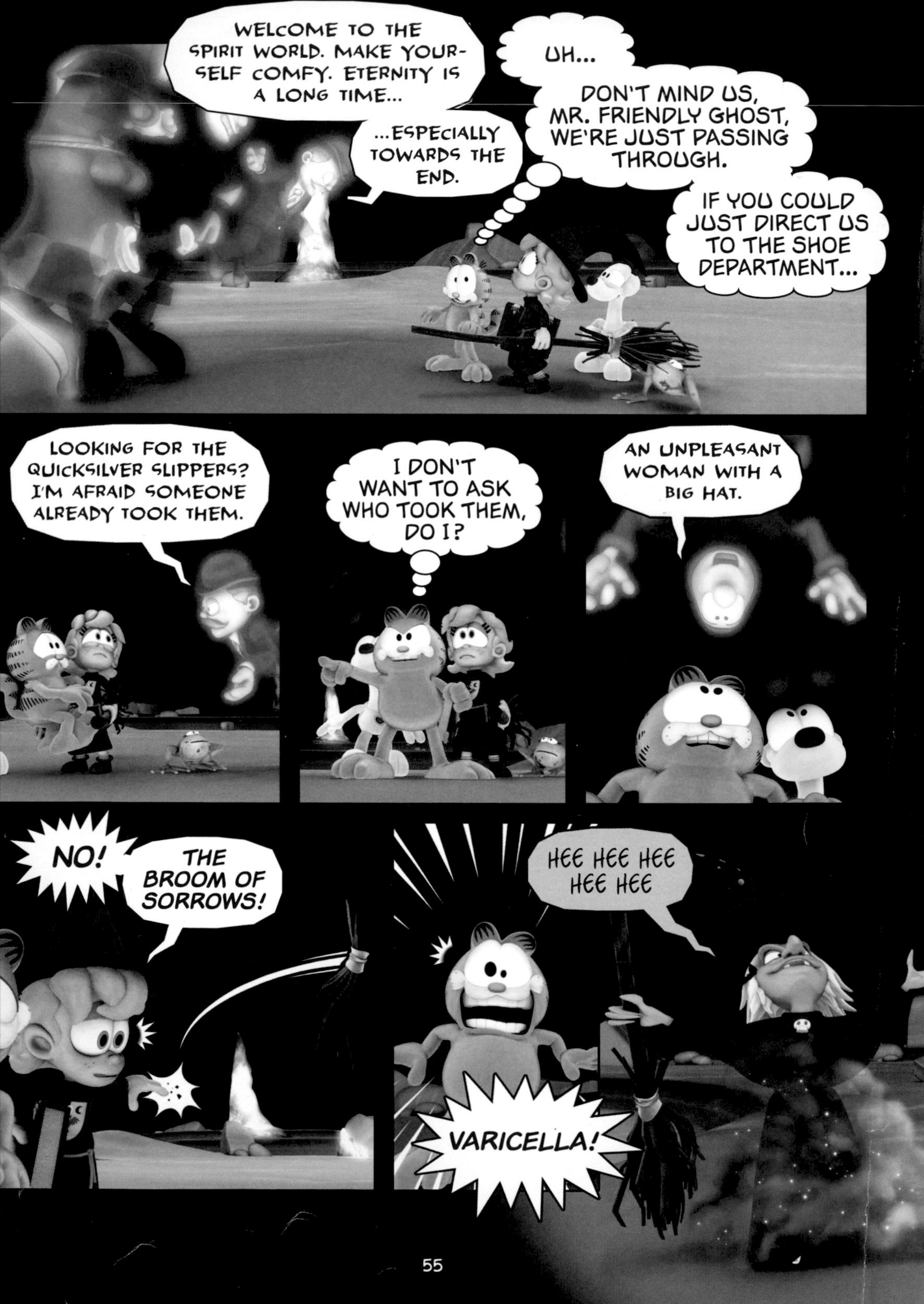
WELCOME TO THE SPIRIT WORLD. MAKE YOURSELF COMFY. ETERNITY IS A LONG TIME...
...ESPECIALLY TOWARDS THE END.
UH...
DON'T MIND US, MR. FRIENDLY GHOST, WE'RE JUST PASSING THROUGH.
IF YOU COULD JUST DIRECT US TO THE SHOE DEPARTMENT...
LOOKING FOR THE QUICKSILVER SLIPPERS? I'M AFRAID SOMEONE ALREADY TOOK THEM.
I DON'T WANT TO ASK WHO TOOK THEM, DO I?
AN UNPLEASANT WOMAN WITH A BIG HAT.
NO!
THE BROOM OF SORROWS!
HEE HEE HEE HEE HEE
VARICELLA!

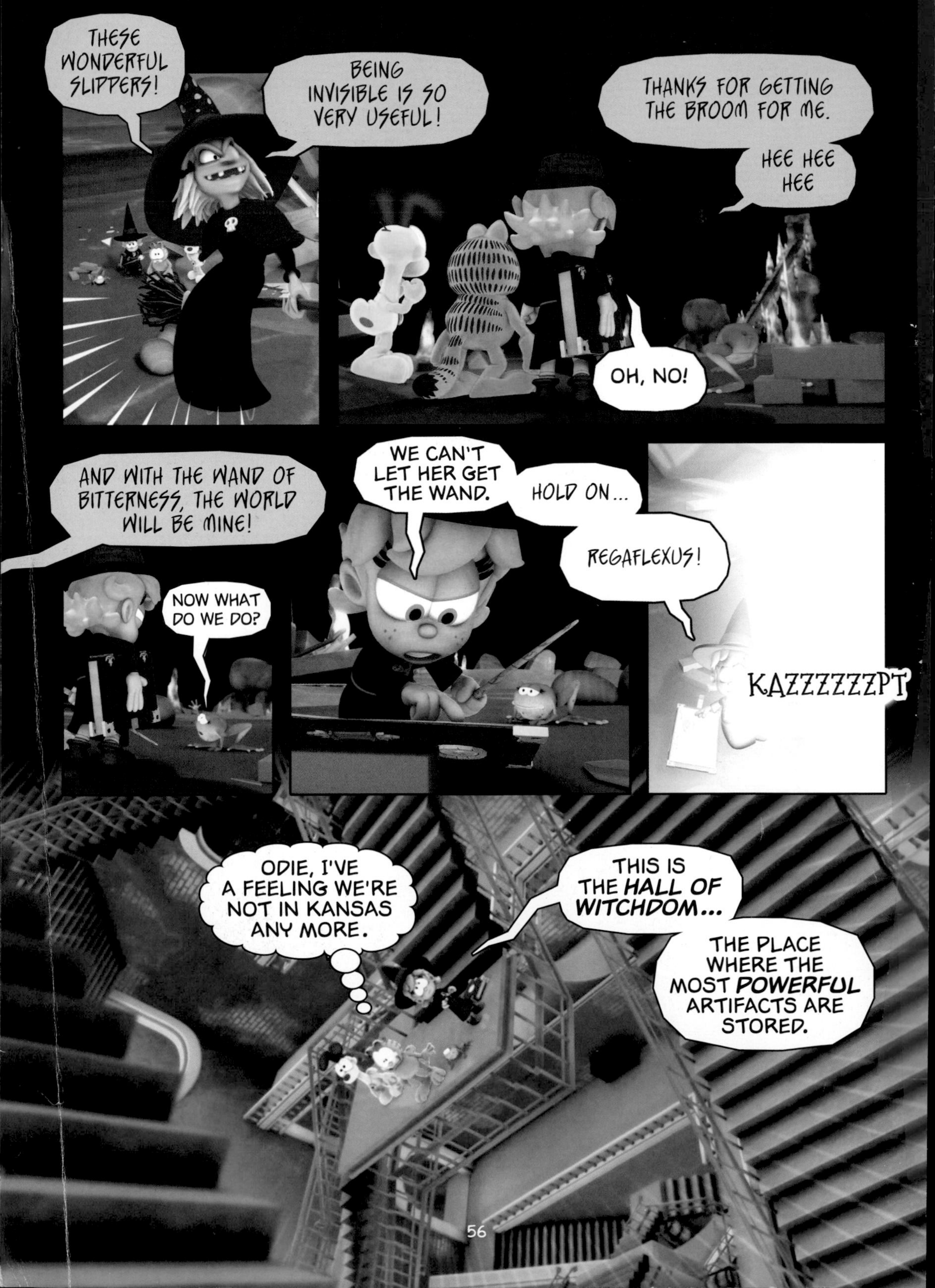
THESE WONDERFUL SLIPPERS!
BEING INVISIBLE IS SO VERY USEFUL!
THANKS FOR GETTING THE BROOM FOR ME.
HEE HEE HEE
OH, NO!
AND WITH THE WAND OF BITTERNESS, THE WORLD WILL BE MINE!
NOW WHAT DO WE DO?
WE CAN'T LET HER GET THE WAND.
HOLD ON...
REGAFLEXUS!
KAZZZZZZPT
ODIE, I'VE A FEELING WE'RE NOT IN KANSAS ANY MORE.
THIS IS THE *HALL OF WITCHDOM*...
THE PLACE WHERE THE MOST *POWERFUL* ARTIFACTS ARE STORED.

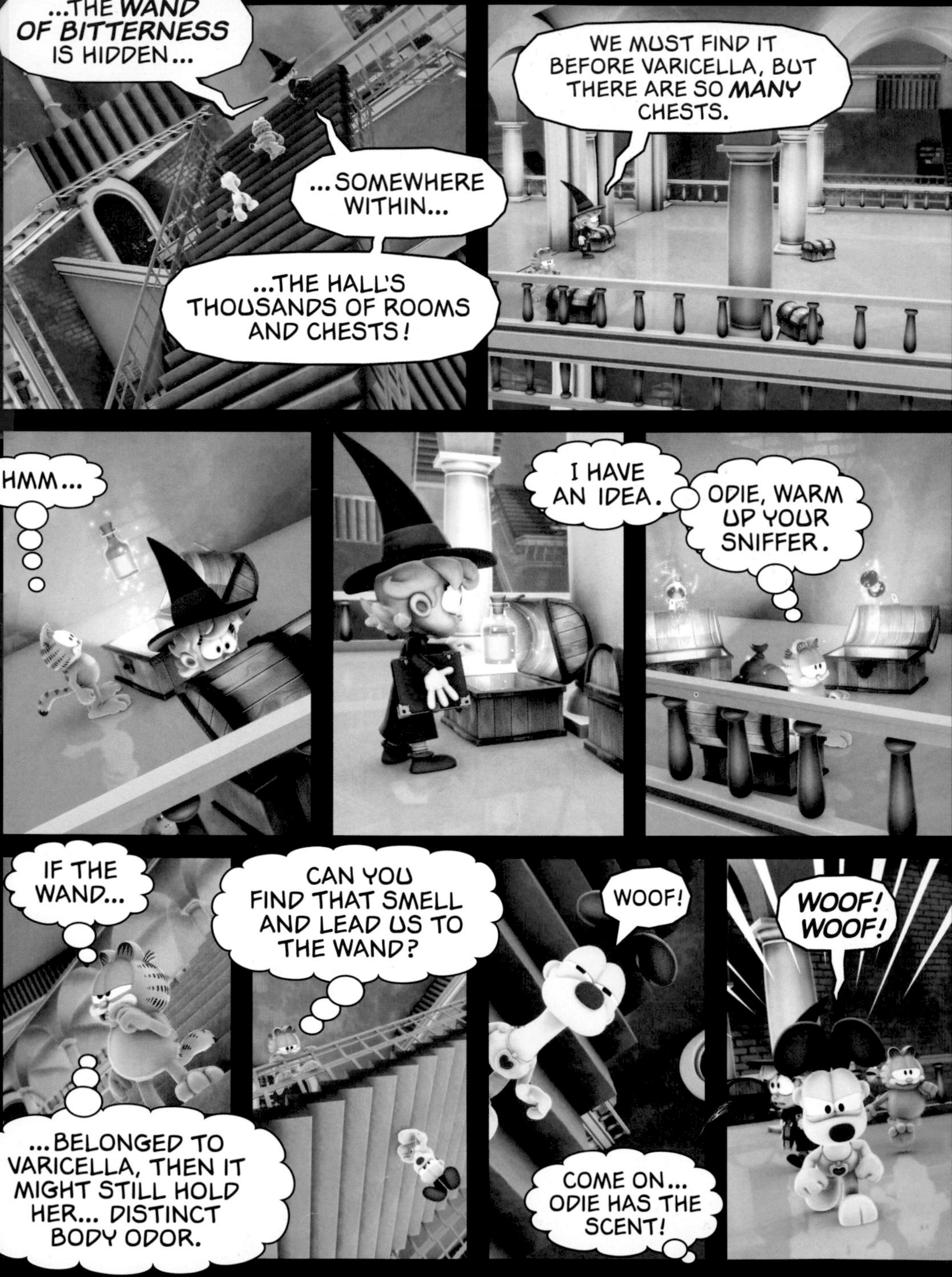

...THE WAND OF BITTERNESS IS HIDDEN...
...SOMEWHERE WITHIN...
...THE HALL'S THOUSANDS OF ROOMS AND CHESTS!
WE MUST FIND IT BEFORE VARICELLA, BUT THERE ARE SO MANY CHESTS.
HMM...
I HAVE AN IDEA.
ODIE, WARM UP YOUR SNIFFER.
IF THE WAND...
...BELONGED TO VARICELLA, THEN IT MIGHT STILL HOLD HER... DISTINCT BODY ODOR.
CAN YOU FIND THAT SMELL AND LEAD US TO THE WAND?
WOOF!
COME ON... ODIE HAS THE SCENT!
WOOF! WOOF!

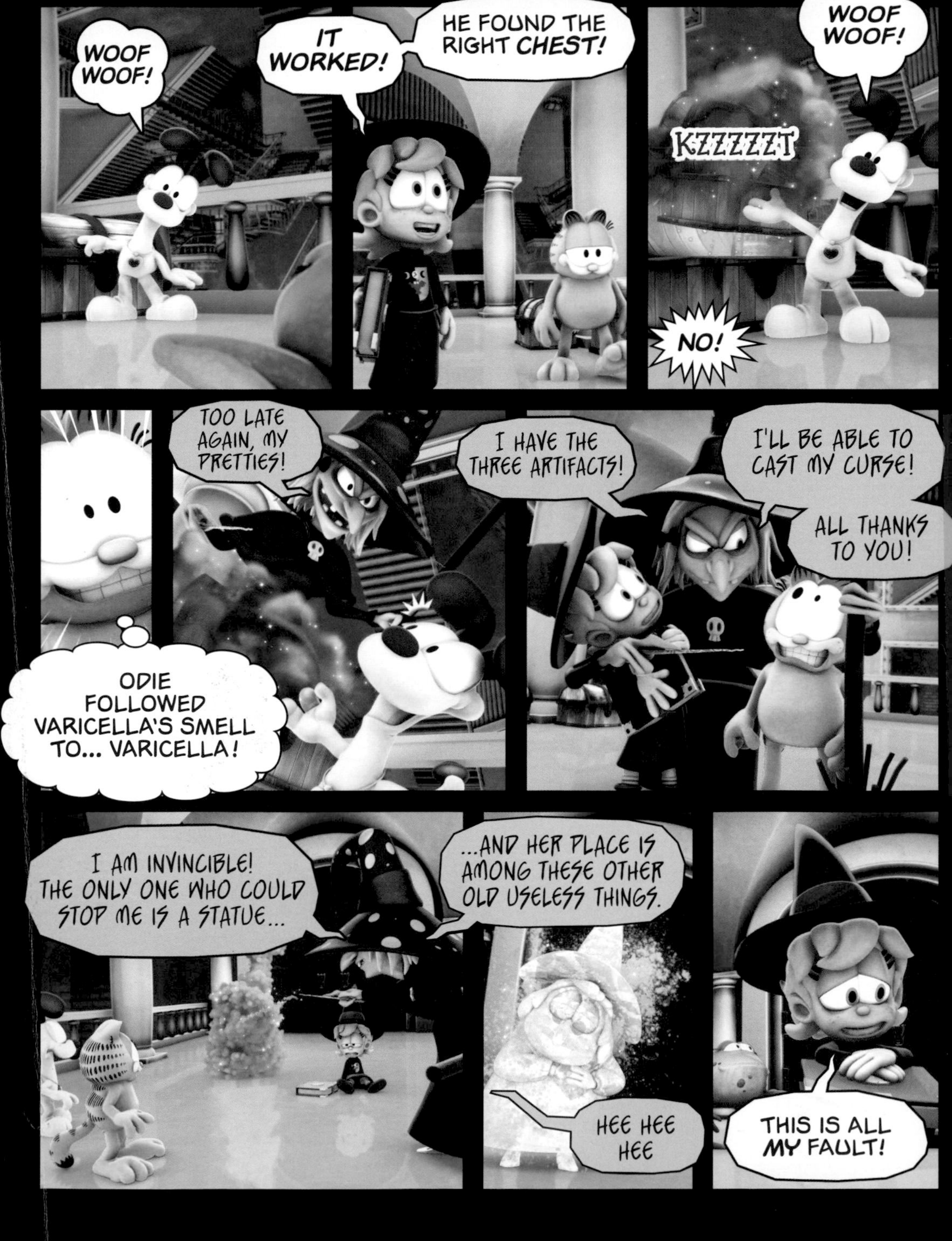
WOOF WOOF!
IT WORKED!
HE FOUND THE RIGHT CHEST!
WOOF WOOF!
KZZZZZT
NO!
ODIE FOLLOWED VARICELLA'S SMELL TO... VARICELLA!
TOO LATE AGAIN, MY PRETTIES!
I HAVE THE THREE ARTIFACTS!
I'LL BE ABLE TO CAST MY CURSE!
ALL THANKS TO YOU!
I AM INVINCIBLE! THE ONLY ONE WHO COULD STOP ME IS A STATUE...
...AND HER PLACE IS AMONG THESE OTHER OLD USELESS THINGS.
HEE HEE HEE
THIS IS ALL MY FAULT!

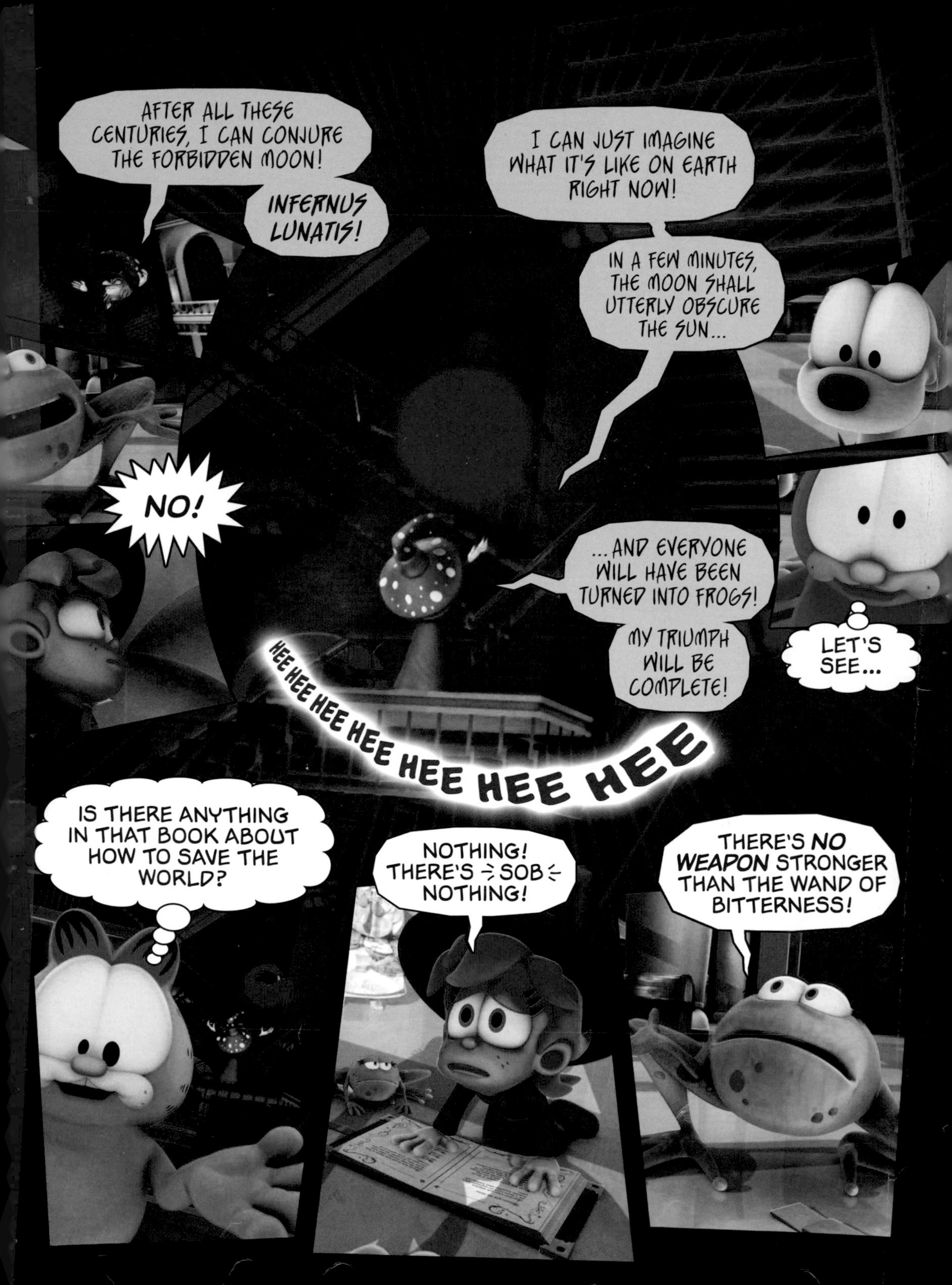
AFTER ALL THESE CENTURIES, I CAN CONJURE THE FORBIDDEN MOON!
INFERNUS LUNATIS!
I CAN JUST IMAGINE WHAT IT'S LIKE ON EARTH RIGHT NOW!
IN A FEW MINUTES, THE MOON SHALL UTTERLY OBSCURE THE SUN...
NO!
...AND EVERYONE WILL HAVE BEEN TURNED INTO FROGS!
MY TRIUMPH WILL BE COMPLETE!
LET'S SEE...
HEE HEE HEE HEE HEE HEE HEE HEE
IS THERE ANYTHING IN THAT BOOK ABOUT HOW TO SAVE THE WORLD?
NOTHING! THERE'S ⇒SOB⇐ NOTHING!
THERE'S NO WEAPON STRONGER THAN THE WAND OF BITTERNESS!

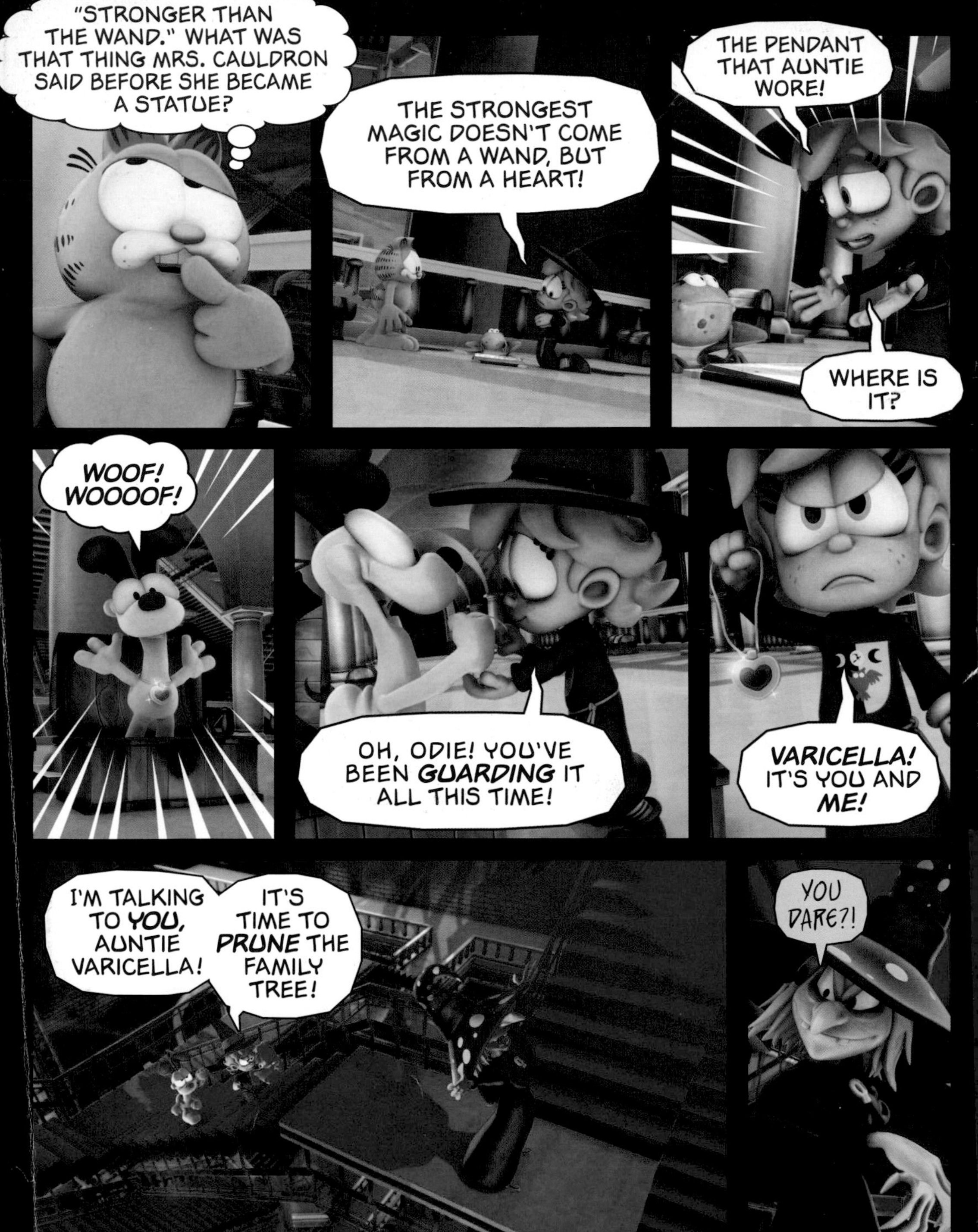
"STRONGER THAN THE WAND." WHAT WAS THAT THING MRS. CAULDRON SAID BEFORE SHE BECAME A STATUE?
THE STRONGEST MAGIC DOESN'T COME FROM A WAND, BUT FROM A HEART!
THE PENDANT THAT AUNTIE WORE!
WHERE IS IT?
WOOF! WOOOOF!
OH, ODIE! YOU'VE BEEN GUARDING IT ALL THIS TIME!
VARICELLA! IT'S YOU AND ME!
I'M TALKING TO YOU, AUNTIE VARICELLA!
IT'S TIME TO PRUNE THE FAMILY TREE!
YOU DARE?!

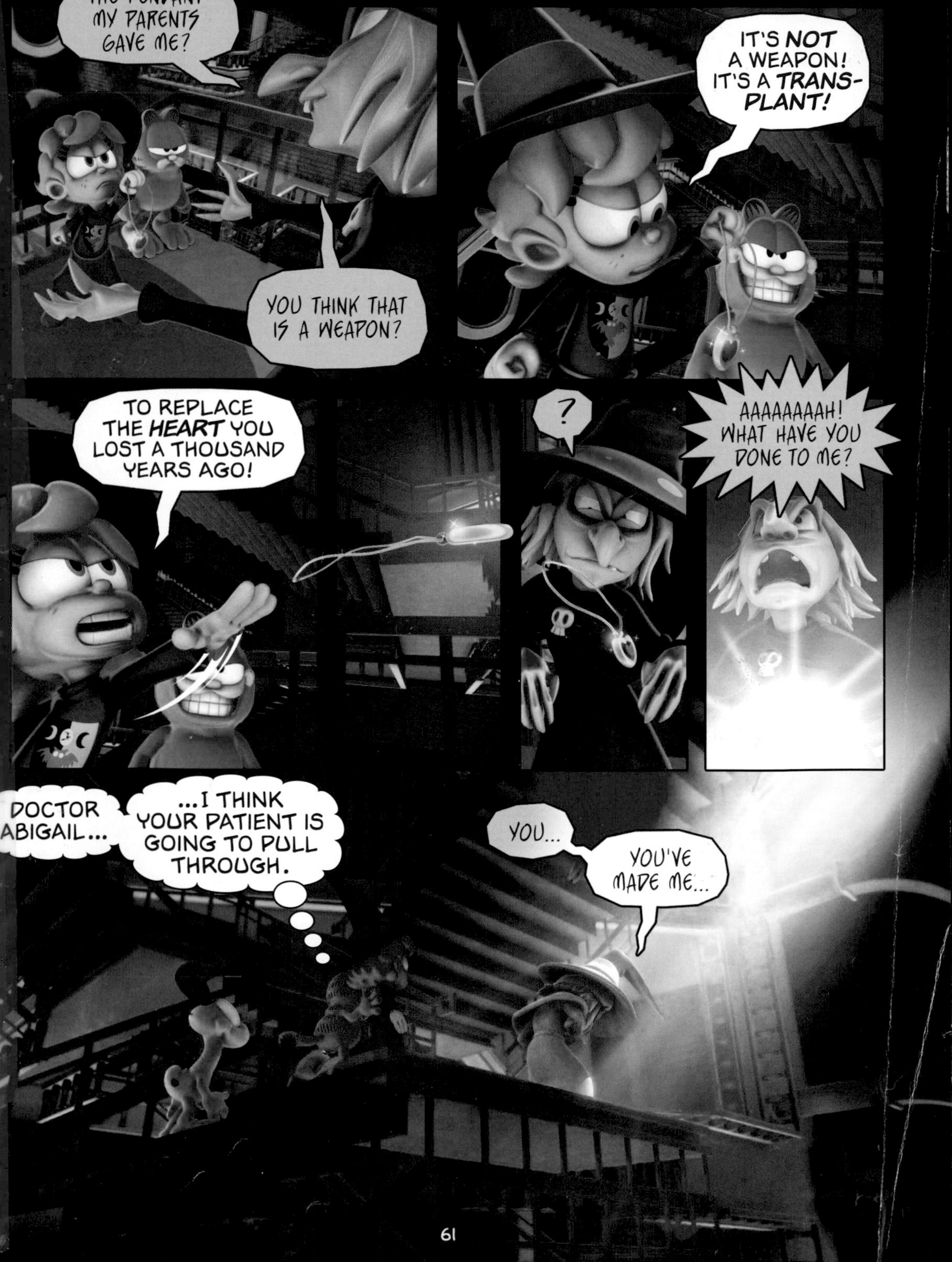

THE PENDANT MY PARENTS GAVE ME?
YOU THINK THAT IS A WEAPON?
IT'S NOT A WEAPON! IT'S A TRANS-PLANT!
TO REPLACE THE HEART YOU LOST A THOUSAND YEARS AGO!
?
AAAAAAAAH! WHAT HAVE YOU DONE TO ME?
DOCTOR ABIGAIL...
...I THINK YOUR PATIENT IS GOING TO PULL THROUGH.
YOU...
YOU'VE MADE ME...

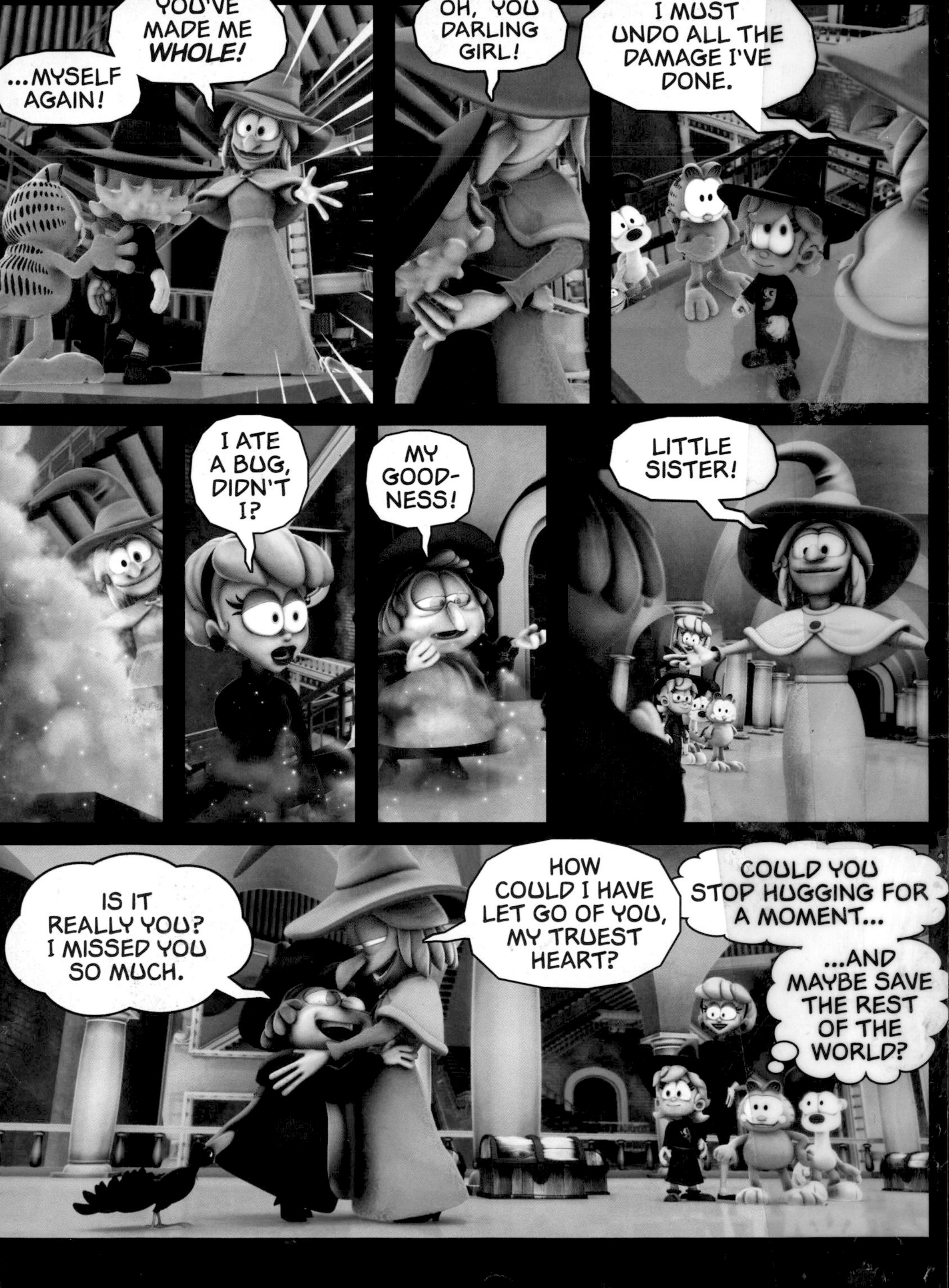
...MYSELF AGAIN!
YOU'VE MADE ME *WHOLE!*
OH, YOU DARLING GIRL!
I MUST UNDO ALL THE DAMAGE I'VE DONE.
I ATE A BUG, DIDN'T I?
MY GOODNESS!
LITTLE SISTER!
IS IT REALLY YOU? I MISSED YOU SO MUCH.
HOW COULD I HAVE LET GO OF YOU, MY TRUEST HEART?
COULD YOU STOP HUGGING FOR A MOMENT...
...AND MAYBE SAVE THE REST OF THE WORLD?

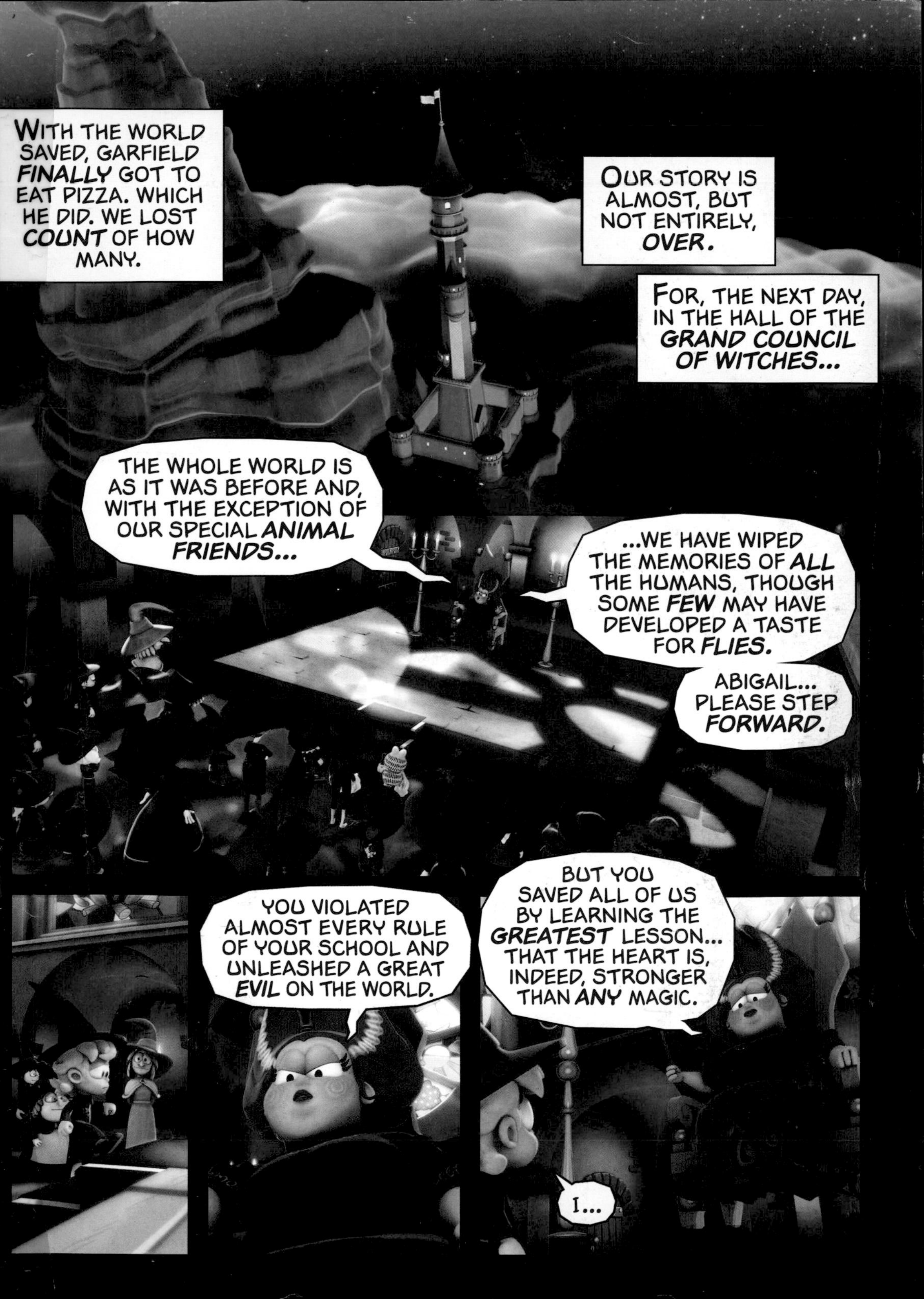
WITH THE WORLD SAVED, GARFIELD FINALLY GOT TO EAT PIZZA. WHICH HE DID. WE LOST COUNT OF HOW MANY.
OUR STORY IS ALMOST, BUT NOT ENTIRELY, OVER.
FOR, THE NEXT DAY, IN THE HALL OF THE GRAND COUNCIL OF WITCHES...
THE WHOLE WORLD IS AS IT WAS BEFORE AND, WITH THE EXCEPTION OF OUR SPECIAL ANIMAL FRIENDS...
...WE HAVE WIPED THE MEMORIES OF ALL THE HUMANS, THOUGH SOME FEW MAY HAVE DEVELOPED A TASTE FOR FLIES.
ABIGAIL... PLEASE STEP FORWARD.
YOU VIOLATED ALMOST EVERY RULE OF YOUR SCHOOL AND UNLEASHED A GREAT EVIL ON THE WORLD.
BUT YOU SAVED ALL OF US BY LEARNING THE GREATEST LESSON... THAT THE HEART IS, INDEED, STRONGER THAN ANY MAGIC.
I...

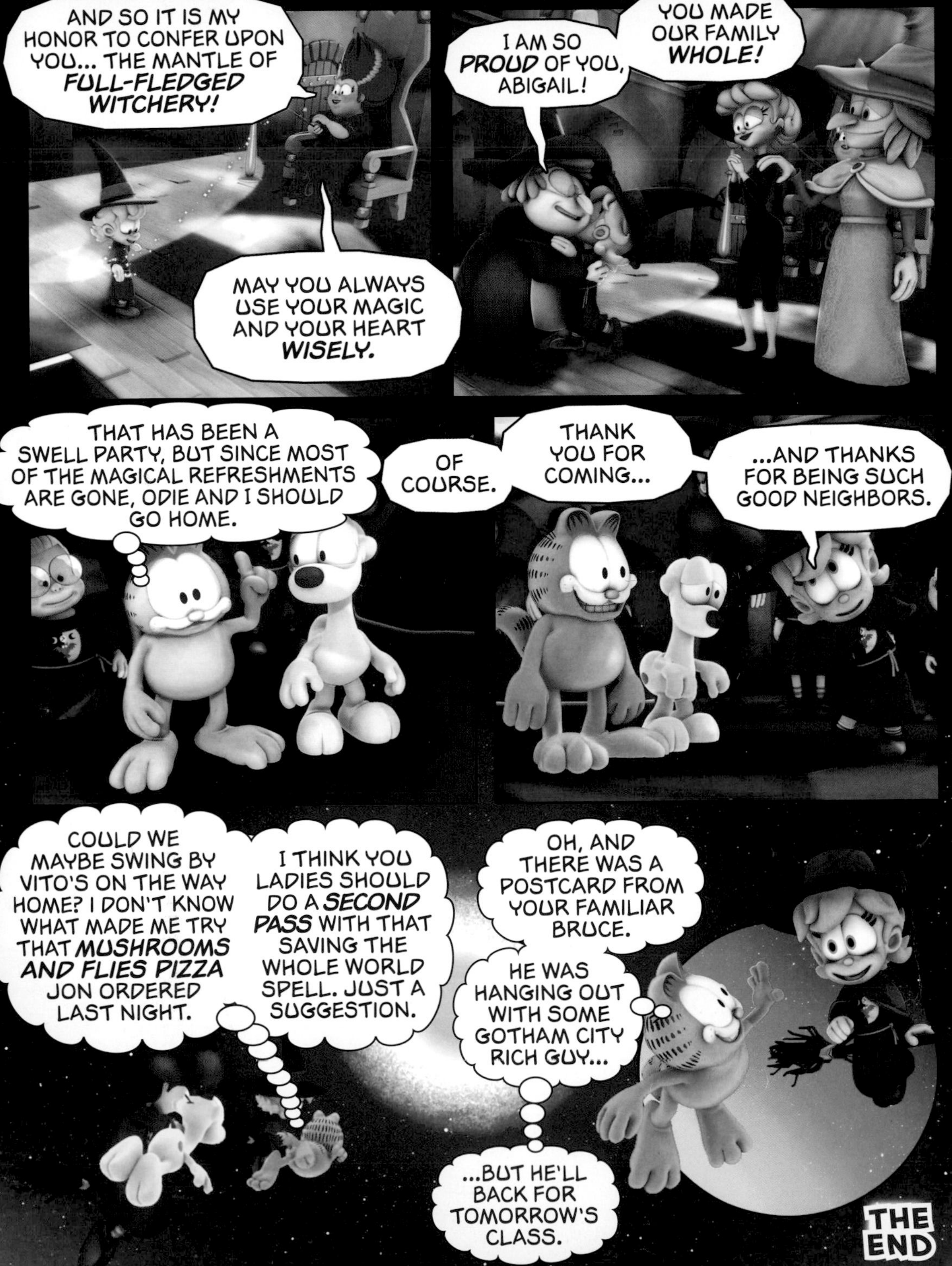
AND SO IT IS MY HONOR TO CONFER UPON YOU... THE MANTLE OF FULL-FLEDGED WITCHERY!
MAY YOU ALWAYS USE YOUR MAGIC AND YOUR HEART WISELY.
I AM SO PROUD OF YOU, ABIGAIL!
YOU MADE OUR FAMILY WHOLE!
THAT HAS BEEN A SWELL PARTY, BUT SINCE MOST OF THE MAGICAL REFRESHMENTS ARE GONE, ODIE AND I SHOULD GO HOME.
OF COURSE.
THANK YOU FOR COMING...
...AND THANKS FOR BEING SUCH GOOD NEIGHBORS.
COULD WE MAYBE SWING BY VITO'S ON THE WAY HOME? I DON'T KNOW WHAT MADE ME TRY THAT MUSHROOMS AND FLIES PIZZA JON ORDERED LAST NIGHT.
I THINK YOU LADIES SHOULD DO A SECOND PASS WITH THAT SAVING THE WHOLE WORLD SPELL. JUST A SUGGESTION.
OH, AND THERE WAS A POSTCARD FROM YOUR FAMILIAR BRUCE.
HE WAS HANGING OUT WITH SOME GOTHAM CITY RICH GUY...
...BUT HE'LL BACK FOR TOMORROW'S CLASS.
THE END